HOW TO CATCH YOUR MAN AND KEEP HIM FOR LIFE

The Greatest Secrets of Men Revealed

EMMANUEL NNAJI

TABLE OF CONTENTS

PREFACE

How to Catch your man and keep Him for life.

What a title for a book! Strange as it may seem, this is the hottest topic in today's contemporary world of relationship experiences. It is easy to observe how easily vulnerable women have become in some relationships with the opposite sex. It seems some men has been destined to continue to have the upper hand, to exploit the love of a woman, and to dump her when they deem it necessary. The cards seem to be stacked against the women. First, they are regarded as the weaker vessels. Surviving in a world where might appears to be right and where strength seems to prevail puts her in a precarious situation, where she must sometimes be at her wits' end to survive. In this "man's world," most women have become more like second fiddlers, relegated to the role of second-class citizens, suitable only for sexual escapades and other meager purposes.

In most societies, it is normal for women to be treated as enslaved people, household properties acquired for pleasure and procreation, and nothing more. Her opinion is not sought in matters of importance, and even when she offers it, it is trampled upon and mocked. **It is dangerous for any society to underrate and therefore despise the role of the woman.** She is more than just a woman.

My purpose in writing this book is to tell every woman that she is a valuable creature, created by God for the good of mankind, even as man was created for the good of the woman too. Yes, woman is good, suitable for man. Men cannot live without women. Even God saw this when He said, **"It is not good that**

the man should be alone... I will make Him a help meet for him." Gen 2:18.

According to the bible, God built woman with man in mind. To help man, God made a woman. She has what it takes to make life worth living for the man she loves. She is a blessing to him. **She is to be loved, respected, cherished, nourished, and valued.** This is God's intent.

This book is motivated by my desire to address specific issues that often arise as I minister to women, particularly concerning relationship management. Many women appear to lack adequate training and education on how to effectively navigate their relationships with men. This knowledge gap is often at the root of many relationship problems..

To drive a car, people typically attend a driving school to learn the skills necessary for safe driving. They don't just get into a car and drive off. To fly a plane, you go to a flight training school. We attend school to acquire knowledge in various areas of skill and discipline. Even when you acquire a new electronic device, you need to study the instruction manual before being able to operate it. Why do we have no problems with going to school to learn how to fly a plane, but we find it odd that we have to undergo some training and education to manage and succeed in a relationship? Just like flying a plane, you need training to handle a man. The same way, men need training to know how to relate with women.

You cannot control what you do not understand. You need knowledge about men to know how best to handle them. This book reveals all the hidden secrets of men; by these, you can never again suffer as a victim of a bad relationship. I will teach you how to recognize the right type of man; how to read his thoughts and respond to him effectively. I will show you major relationship mistakes women make that cost them their engagements and sometimes, their marriages. This book is the training you need to fly this "jet" called man. Before ever getting into a relationship with a man, you need to gather as much information as you can about them. It is easy to catch your man and keep him for life. All you need is to be able to enter a man's mind and see how he thinks, how he feels about certain things women do, the things that scare him in a woman. Why do they run away from making major marital commitments? You need a man to help you find that out. That is exactly what I am doing. I am a man. I can tell you a few things about men. Perhaps this will help you in your next relationship, if you're not in one already. If you're already in a relationship, you have the opportunity to sidestep those "silly" blunders that many women tend to make, which can unexpectedly drive the man away. By being mindful, you can strengthen your connection and keep the spark alive.

Do you feel your relationship is becoming stale and the romance is gone? Not to worry, this book opens for you a new river of romantic possibilities only available to those who seek. Jesus said, **"Seek and you shall find..." Matthew. 7:7.**

Hey there! I just want to reach out to all the amazing women out there because I truly care about you. I want to see you happy and smiling, and I'm excited to share some timeless secrets that can help you attract and keep the right partner. You're not alone in this journey!

I will also show you how to deal with the competition. All it takes is the correct information. I have conducted extensive research on this topic, spanning several years of study and counseling. I have discussed this with many men. I ask them questions like: "What do you want in a woman?" "What does a woman need to do to keep you for life?" "What could make you fall in love instantly with a woman?" These are among the questions I ask them. I also look within myself to seek answers to these questions. They have provided me with answers that have shaped the plot of this book. For example, when you ask any man what he wants in a woman, here are some of the answers you get:

1. They want a submissive woman. Not challenging their authority. Not a robot but one who respects them.
2. They want a beautiful woman. One, they can take home to their parents proudly.
3. They want a woman who fears God. Well behaved.
4. They want a woman who is not afraid to work. Not a lazy bird. One who can be a partner in life struggles and wins.
5. They want a woman who looks and smells clean.
6. They want a woman who is cheerful, loving, and forgiving. One who speaks well of people.
7. They also want a woman who can give them kids. Well this applies to those who are thinking about their legacies.

In the section "Laws of Seduction" I revealed hidden secrets that every woman must know about men. How to get into his world by first getting into his mind and having him think about you till he falls madly in love with you!

I will show you how to set the stage to make him chase after you as God told Adam to *"cleave"* unto his wife. The word "cleave" actually means to pursue after; to chase. He is meant to be chasing you, not you chasing him. This book guides you on the journey to become the captivating woman he desires.

Who said good men are scarce? They are not scarce; they are everywhere. You need to know where to find them. Make this book your best companion and relationship consultant, and see the tables turn in all your affairs with men.

This is your finest moment – seize it!

INTRODUCTION

Jesus looked down at Peter and said these words: "Do not be afraid, from now on, you will catch men" Luke 5:10 "From henceforth, thou shalt catch men". (KJV).

I didn't start this whole concept of catching men; God started it. It is His will to teach us how to catch men. Men are likened to fish. You need to study them thoroughly to know how to catch them. One law of fishing is *the bait principle.* To catch fish, you need the right bait. This book is written for the woman who needs to know what it takes to locate her man, her God-given mate, catch him (or get him to catch her), and keep him for life.

Fish come in a variety of sizes and shapes. To be successful in fishing, you must know the fish you are trying to catch. Peter was to adopt, in fishing for men, the same strategy he used in fishing: the same strategies, but a different target. If you are a woman seeking truth on these lines, you are reading the right book! Herein, you will find all the secrets of the game of **men-hunting**. Why write a book on how to catch a man? Are men animals to be caught? No. But just as in hunting, every hunter knows something about the game he is trying to catch.

You need to know about men so that you don't fall victim to what most women experience today: heartbreaks, divorces, separation, betrayal, two-timing (unfaithfulness), the list goes on. Every woman is destined for her God-given mate, a man who complements her soul. Yet, far too often, the absence of guidance in understanding and navigating relationships leads to heartache when love takes an unfortunate turn. As a counseling Minister, I counsel single and married women who come to seek counsel on relationship problems. From "why doesn't he love me anymore?" to "Why did he leave me? It was so great at first…" I see in these women seeking relationship advice, the same pattern repeating itself over and over again. First, love or infatuation, then intimacy, and then rejection. What is it in a strange woman that makes a man leave his woman for her? Why do men cheat? (Well, not all men). How can a woman catch her man and keep him for life? What are the boundaries that exist for seduction? Can a woman use her seductive power legally? What are the secret laws of seduction that can guarantee a lifelong relationship filled with bliss? Are there things about men women need to know? Maybe things that their men find difficult to tell them about themselves? For example, a non-verbal person is not necessarily a tolerant and nice person. He's just not talking about how he really feels. Are there other ways to decide what he is trying to tell you? Can love truly last forever? Is there hope even after everything is broken and lost?

In this book, I treat all these issues and much more. You will learn the 16 things all women need to know about men. Knowing your catch is crucial to having a successful hunting expedition. You will discover the secrets to locating your ideal partner and setting the stage for him to come looking for you. You will learn how the predator is the prey and the prey the predator. You will also learn the 11 things never to do with a man. These things are the fastest ways to lose a man. You will also be trained on how to identify potential competition, such as another woman, and how to address it at the root. I will show you why you must never get too emotional about him, or at least don't show it. Once a man thinks that you are crazy about him, your influence over him begins to wane. Keep him hunting for a game (game: that which is hunted);

one he may never catch. Keep him coming back for you. Keep him dependent on you. Keep him. I will show you how.

LET'S GO FISHING

Chapter One

TO CATCH A FISH

Know your fish: Let us begin this book by conducting a brief study on fishing. Just as Jesus said to Peter, ***"Follow me and I will make you fishers of men" (Matt. 4:19),*** it is clear that, like fish, catching men requires strategy. There appears to be a correlation in the behavior patterns of humans and fish. Just like fish, humans need bait to be caught. What is a bait? It is food used to trap or lure animals or fish, serving as an enticement to tease.

A desire for gain naturally drives human beings. Once we see that we can gain from something, we go for it, sometimes damning the consequences. That is what I believe the devil saw in man when he lured him out of the will of God, and made him eat the apple which God had told him not to eat. **Gen 2:17.** In fact, God even said that he would die on the day he ate the fruit. Man was fully aware of this fact when the devil came, dangling before his eyes the bait of everlasting life, wisdom, and equality with God **(Genesis 3:4,5)**. The serpent used the bait principle, and man, knowing full well the consequences of his action, went on and did what God said not to do – he ate the forbidden fruit.

A Bait can be so powerful. It can blind the eyes of reason and shut the ears from hearing the sound of danger. Once the mind of man is lured into that bait, like the fish, not minding the hook hidden under the bait, puts its mouth to take the bait and is hooked.

Jesus was saying to Peter, *"To catch men, you need to use the same methods you use in fishing; Use baits."* Jesus used a lot of baits. First, He knew man. He knew what men wanted. He knew all their hopes, aspirations, secret passions, and proclivities. He understood d man. He knew that to catch a man, you must give him what he wants and use that to put your hook on him. Once he bites the hook, there is no escaping. He is captured.

So we need a little education on fishing if we are going to be good catchers.

There are five basic principles about fishing.

Principle 1: Know what you are fishing for

As a woman seeking a man, you have been told you need to think like a fisherman (or woman). What type of "fish" are you looking for? If you don't know the kind of "fish" you are looking for, how will you know when you catch it? In nature, there are various types of fish. And every kind of fish has its strategy for catching it. That is to say, you can't use what works for fish "A" to catch fish "B"; it won't work. Talking about actual fish, there are kinds of fish; there is the catfish, the bass, the salmon, the marlin, and the trout. Each fish requires different equipment, bait, and timing. The type of fish you are trying to catch will determine the strategy you must adopt. There is no "one–size–fits–all " strategy to fishing. So, do you know the "fish" you are trying to catch? In one of the chapters, I discussed the various types of men.

Men are different; what works for one person may not work for another. As our faces are different, so are we in character, likes, dislikes, choices, and behavior. So in your quest for your man, narrow your target to the type of man you were designed to catch. You can't attract and keep every man. That is impossible. You don't appeal to every man you meet. Some may find you attractive, some may not. Accept it, and don't take it personally. You are best equipped to catch your type, men whose type you are. Men of your class and experience. So, the first principle is that you must know your kind of "fish" (by "fish" here, I use it as a metaphor for man). Who you are is who you attract.

Principle 2: Go where the fish are biting

Every fish has its bait. Not all fish will bite a particular bait. There are fish you can't catch with a line and hook. They may require a net or a fishing machine. To catch your fish, go where the fish are biting. Don't waste your time fishing where the fish are not biting. Be flexible and ready to adapt. A skilled fisherman knows that fish feed at different locations at various times of the day. Neither are they hungry all the time. This is why I believe Jesus told Peter, ***"Launch out into the deep for a great catch" (Luke 5:4).*** Be ready to go where the fish are. To catch serious fish, you can't stick yourself to one spot, expecting them to come to you. Go to them first, and soon they will come looking for you. Fish want to be caught on their terms. If you are not received or accepted at one spot, move on to the next place. Nothing spectacular can be caught in the shallow water. Get out there into the deep. Don't hang around a place where you are abused and not valued when there is another place in the same lake of men where you will be treated like the queen you are. Has any "fish" rejected your bait? Don't take it personally, it's not your fault, it's just that it is not your type of fish. To catch fish, you must be willing to change your strategy and go where the fish are biting – where you are needed.

Principle 3: Learn to think like a fish

To catch a fish, you must think like a fish. You must understand their habits, preferences, and feeding patterns. It takes close and analytical studying to learn to think like a fish. If you are a woman, you must learn to think like a man. Get into their minds to get into their world. Think like a fish to catch a fish. For example, some fish prefer smooth, still water, and others like to swim in rushing rivers. Some fish prefer a life that is cool, easy, and predictable, while others prefer to live on the wild side. Some fish like to hide under rocks while others are bottom crawlers. Men, like fish, are unique.

Studying fish helps you understand how they think. Knowing how he thinks enables you to understand precisely what you can do to attract him. Study him. The heart is revealed in words, actions, gestures, facial expressions, humor, rage, likes and dislikes, body movements, eye contact, where one goes, and with whom one relates, among other things.

Women often become frustrated when interacting with men due to this issue; they don't spend time studying men. They assume that all men are the same. That is a fatal error. You can't control what you don't understand. To help you with this, I will address it in subsequent chapters.

Principle 4: Catch the fish on their terms

Fish are self-willed creatures. No fish goes out of its place expecting to be caught that day. So don't expect them to cooperate with you. If anything, they will try their best to take your bait and escape out of your reach. This is the stark reality of fishing: no fish wants to be caught. You can't catch fish by preparing a stove with a pot of boiling oil and say *"O fishy fishy fishy! Jump out of the water into my pot!"* No fish will do that. To be successful in fishing, you must be willing to catch fish on their terms. You must be willing to do whatever it takes to get them. You must be serious about catching fish, serious enough to launch out into the deep as Jesus told Peter. It will require you to make personal changes to become what they are looking for. There is who you need to be to catch who you want to catch.

Ask yourself these questions: Am I willing to:

a. Understand and adapt to their culture?

It is said that when you are in Rome, behave like the Romans. But don't lose your identity. It's a man's world but to thrive in this world, you must be ready to adapt to man's culture. Try to think like a man. Drop that weakling, vulnerable, and powerless role the world has forced on women. Women are not weak and vulnerable creatures, needing to be rescued. It is learning to adapt to man's culture that protects women from being seen as creatures of abuse to be preyed upon at will. What a man needs is another man in the body of a woman! Someone like him, someone he can talk with, reason with, go out with, hang out with, play with, and exchange ideas with. You can be a man by thinking like one; after all, the word "woman" has "man" in it. A woman is simply a man with a womb! She is everything a man is plus more. So she can be like a man. Get into the man's life and occupy the void, and he won't need to seek another. Not even fellow men.

b. Am I willing to let my target determine my approach?

As we have stressed in this chapter, you can't use a one–size–fits–all approach for every person you meet. People are different. What one person may find funny, another may find very offensive. Like Paul in 1 Corinthians 9:19-22, you must be adaptable. Be all things to all to catch some. Are you prepared to change for that "fish" you are trying to catch?

c. Am I prepared to meet their needs?

Every man has a need. A want. A hidden pain. A bad experience. An unhealed wound. An unfulfilled dream. A regret. A vision. How can you meet some of these needs? This is very crucial. We will talk more about this in the chapters ahead. Are you willing to overlook his weaknesses, problems, and habits as you attempt to help him change? Are you prepared to change what you can in a man and accept the ones you can't change? Do you have a solution to man's needs?

Every man needs:

- To be loved
- To be respected
- To be appreciated
- To be respected and valued
- To be listened to
- f. To be pampered like a baby.
- g. To be treated with importance in public.
- h. To be sexually fulfilled.

The list goes on. Can you solve his problems? Can you meet these needs?

d. Am I willing to understand and respond to wrong impressions men have of women?

The reason some men are acting the way they do to women may be because of the hang-ups they have about women. A bad experience with love in the past can turn a man into an animal seeking whom he may devour in revenge. To be successful in catching men, you must be very sensitive about how they think about women. Most men do not respect women; no wonder they continue to treat some of them like whores. To some men, women are mere sex objects to execute their sexual and carnal urges, nothing more. Be conscious of this and seek to change that impression. Make a difference. The way you behave in your relationship with a man can affect the way that man views women, either positively or negatively. See yourself as an ambassador of Eve. You are not inferior to man. You were created to help him. This is huge! It means he can't do without you. Yes, it is a man's world, but it will mean nothing without a woman in it.

In the next chapter, we will study man as a subject so that we can know how to catch him and keep him for life.

Principle 5: Use more than one hook

Be flexible to be effective in fishing. Have an arsenal of tools and strategies. Prepare yourself by acquiring all the equipment, training, and skills you may need. Have something for everyone.

LETS TALK ABOUT MEN

Chapter Two

KNOW YOUR MAN

In the last chapter, we saw that you cannot control what you don't understand or know very well. You are a victim of what you don't know. To catch a man and keep him for life, you must understand him. In this chapter, I will show you some of the character traits of men. I will show you what a man is like outside God, the unregenerated man. You will see that it takes the nature and life of God actively working in a person to make them the warm, friendly person you want them to be.

MAN IS A RULER

So we ask Who is Man? To answer this question, we go back to His creator. Man did not create himself; God created man. **"And God said, Let us make man in Our image, after Our likeness. Let them have dominion over the fish of the sea..." Genesis 1:26.** From this verse, we can see that man was made to rule. He is a ruler. He has a mandate to exercise rulership. That is why he does not take it kindly when his ego is trampled upon. In catching men, you must bear that in mind. He is a king. God designed it to be so. To the woman, God said, **"I will greatly multiply thy sorrow and thy conception; in sorrow thou shalt bring forth children: and thy desire shall be to thy husband, and he shall rule over thee". Gen 3:16.** He shall rule over thee. This statement came to the woman as a result of the fall. From then on, God gave woman her position in the family. She is to submit herself to her husband. He is to rule over her.

Man thinks like a ruler. He sees himself as superior (in rank) to the woman. Regardless of your feelings on the matter, this is the reality. With all the noise about sexual equality, the fact is that it is a man–ruled world. Look around you, and you will notice that men, in general, rule. As a woman seeking to attract and retain a man, you must acknowledge this fact. You are dealing with someone who views himself as superior to women in rank. Even in the home, God established this to be so. He told us in the book of Ephesians 5:22 23 **"Wives submit yourselves unto your own husbands, as unto the Lord." Why? "For the husband is the head of the wife, even as Christ is the head of the church."** You can't conquer a man by confrontation. When you refuse to recognize his God given authority over you, you lose out totally. He will do everything to protect his position and enforce his rule because that is how he has been made to see himself. Even if circumstances handicap him, he thinks about acquiring his kingdom and authority, and most of the time, it forms the motivation that drives him to pursue power and significance. Man is a natural ruler. So is the woman also.

Because of man's inherent need for respect and affirmation, he attaches great importance to power in all its ramifications. This is the driving force behind his quest for wealth. He wants to show everyone who he is. How do you catch a man? Find what he wants and give it to him. Let him have authority and rulership. Once he ceases to see you as a threat to his authority, he becomes powerless. Acknowledging his power is your power over him. Subdue him with absolute submission. Submission creates something more powerful than power and authority: Influence. Most times, it is not the king who decides what happens in the realm. It is the people influencing him. Don't fight the king; submit to his kingdom, and he will forfeit the will to act as king to you. While God gave man authority and rulership, He gave woman influence.

Influence is more powerful than power itself. To understand man, you must first realize (1) who created him: God. (2) What he created him to be. He was created to rule. He is not to exercise dominion over women as though women were another inferior animal in the garden; he is to respect and protect her and value her as a co–ruler over creation. But in the family hierarchy, he is above the woman. This is the way it is. Work with it.

Now I will list some other things you need to know about the man. You will find these traits in almost every man you encounter.

1. **He is a ruler-** we have stressed this point. Knowing this helps resolve many relationship problems people encounter.

2. **He is a Hunter –** Man is always looking for game to hunt. He is constantly setting traps and devising strategies to catch them. If he is not hunting for food, money, status, power, new clothes, or needs, he is hunting for sex. While you are planning on catching him, he is also planning to catch you. He always sees what he does not yet possess as his next challenge. Once he acquires it, it loses appeal to him. He adds it to his collections and off he goes again for another catch. Most times, women don't need to go out and catch men. Men will find them where they are and try to take them. So, in catching a man, you must learn how not to be caught. You must train yourself never to fall victim to any one of his tricks. Men can do or say anything to get what they want. Don't be fooled. Instead of making yourself a prey, he will hunt and catch and drop, keep him hunting for you eternally. How? Use the same methods he uses on women. The disadvantage of hunting is that while your eyes are set on your catch, you fail to

see that some other person has set a trap for you. Hunters are blind. They only see what they are trying to get. They don't consider for a moment that the hunter could be the hunted. Since you know what he wants, use that as a trap to get what you want out of him without falling into his trap. Hunt the hunter. Use what he is trying to get as your hook. Never give it to him, and never let him think you will never give it to him. He is hooked as long as he has not caught his game. In choosing your man, you must realize that it is up to you and not the hunter to decide the game. You hold the cards. Use it wisely. Hunters are blind. They only see what they are trying to get, never seeing what is trying to get them. So to catch a man, your man, let him think he is doing the hunting. More on this in subsequent chapters

3. **He is extremely cunning:** Man is a brilliant creature. Be wary of this fact. You are not dealing with a fool. He believes he is more intelligent than you. He thinks he has figured you out and can handle you. He prides himself on his mental prowess and is constantly competing and trying to outdo perceived competition. When he is not talking he is thinking. His heart is deceitful and desperately perverse. This is a picture of a man outside God. He is cunning and ruthless. Sometimes when he speaks, he speaks to himself. He asks a question to which he already has an answer. Never underrate the mind of a man. Even when they look like fools, they seldom are. To some, their foolishness is their wisdom. Arm yourself with this knowledge. To catch your man, you must know how to deal with *his mind*. You must invade his thinking by learning to read between the lines of what he says. Listen to what he says and watch what he does. Like a chameleon, he is highly adaptive. He knows how to put on the color of the present moment and try to adapt to the environment. So he may be speaking to you based on how he feels at that moment.

Don't be surprised to see him say something contrary in another situation. To avoid hurt and heartbreak, learn to understand how he thinks. To conquer him, appear less intelligent and naïve. Make him your mentor in life. Ask him to teach you. In time, you will learn all his tricks. No man feels threatened when his intelligence is appreciated and revered. The less complex you appear to him, the less he needs to think when dealing with you. Over time, you have swallowed up his intelligence, and soon he will begin to play the cards you deal out to him. You are now in charge!

4. **He is Self-Centered –** To be self-centered is to be egoistic. To be egoistical. To be egocentric. It means a life limited to doing and caring only about oneself and one's own needs. Man is self-centered. Everything he does is motivated purely by what he will derive from it. He is profit–oriented. Dealing with men must be done with this knowledge. He is out for what he can get out of you, period. He believes the whole world revolves around him and his needs. If it does not please him and address his basic needs, you cannot be certain of his total commitment. How do you win over someone like this? To catch a man, you must be ready to deal with this basic fact. You may say, *"I don't think all men are like that…"* You are very correct. But you are not very informed about the true psychology of men. Even when he is nice to you and gives you gifts, it is because of what he will gain from you. The day you cease to mean anything to him and no longer meet those needs, he walks. He may not walk away physically (as in leaving you), but he walks out emotionally. Suddenly, you realize he is no longer as charming and as friendly as he used to be. This is what accounts for many cases of heartbreak and failed relationships. You failed to realize he wants something you have. Something he believes he can gain from you. So ask yourself, "What can I add to his life? What do I have that he needs? If you

want to keep him, you must meet his egoistic needs. What does he want?

Man's needs are:

a. **Sexual:** Does he find in you the fulfillment of all his sexual imaginations? Are you the woman of his dreams? If you are not, either try to be or forget him and walk away. Are you what *he* wants? Watch what I asked you; I did not ask if he is everything *you* want. Are you everything HE wants? If not, drop him now!

b. **Egoistic:** Do you feed his ego? Do you make him feel good about himself? Do you treat him like the king he sees himself as? Do you make him think that apart from him, there is no other?

c. **Intellectual:** Do you feed his need to grow intellectually? Can he talk to you? Do you understand what he is trying to say, or are you trying to get him to hear what you want him to listen to? Do you value his wisdom? Do you praise his ideas and agree with them? Do you sometimes quote him and make references to his inventive and creative prowess? Can he discuss serious matters with you?

d. **Material:** Man has material needs, too. He wants his needs met. He wants to buy that dream car. Move into that big house in that prestigious neighborhood. He wants to advance in the social hierarchy and acquire material wealth. Somehow, he is relating to you because he believes you can help him achieve these material/ social goals. Either by giving him the money or by helping him get to it. Can you help him achieve his financial goals?

e. **Spiritual:** Do you stir him spiritually? Are there intangible and sublime, esoteric qualities in your personality that exudates that sense of mystery and desire for you? Are you spiritual? Have you dug into your true self to find that treasure in you that was created to make you an asset to all? Have you found God? Has He found you? Have you stepped out of the mundane and predictable into the world of high spiritual ability and attraction? Are you detached from people because of your contentment in God? Do you show qualities of a potential gold mine waiting to be discovered, or are you shallow and easily knowable?

He wants you as long as he cannot have you. So detach yourself and dedicate yourself to developing your spiritual self to the point where you become a mystery, one that no one can break.

f. **Praise:** Man craves praise. He wants people to admire him for something he has that they can't have. He likes to show off. Even when he appears modest and humble, he keeps it inside, but he loves it when he is praised. Are you something he can boast of? Can he take you out and show you off? Are you beautiful? Are you worth all the attention? Can you give him something he can be proud of? Can your life make him feel good in the eyes of others? His friends, his relatives, his neighbors, his enemies? Work on it.

g. **Children:** One central thought a man thinks about is posterity. Who takes after him? He feels he has a mandate to extend or continue the family tree. Put simply, he wants children. He may not always say it to you, but he wants them all the same. Children to him are proof of his ability to reproduce himself. It is a basic creator instinct that lies deep in the fabric of every man's consciousness. He may not want them now, but he wants them. That is the primary reason he is getting married. To raise children in a Godly environment. He wants well-trained, gifted children not for any particular reason, but because it makes him feel good and look good in the eyes of others.

i. **Respect:** He wants respect. This cannot be overemphasized. He wants to feel as if he is something more important to you than any other thing or person in your life. Underneath that pleasant and cheerful exterior is an overriding urge to be in control of something, someone.

This chapter is dedicated to helping you know men better—more in the next chapter.

Other qualities and traits that are common to all men. Men are the same everywhere. They may all look different in terms of color, race, or creed. They are the same in makeup. The difference is in how they express themselves. Never be deceived by the outward man. That is the person you meet, and he is kind, giving, and witty. A man can do almost anything to win a woman's affection. He can become whatever he feels you want him to be. Generally men believe women want them to be who they are not. So they act and change once they come into the presence of someone they find attractive.

Don't get me wrong, I am not implying that they use good works to conceal evil intentions all the time to catch prey. This is not accurate. Some genuine men fall in love with a woman and resolve to make personal changes to please the woman they are trying to win. It is often said that a woman has the power to transform a man, elevating him beyond his baser instincts. But that raises an intriguing question: how frequently do we encounter such remarkable women? Before we continue with that thought, let's see the other traits of a natural man. We are not saying he cannot change; he can if he finds the right woman. In the previous chapter, we saw that he is (i) A Ruler, (ii) a hunter, (iii) extremely cunning, and (iv) self-centered and egoistic.

We will proceed to the 5th trait of this gender, called man.

Every Superman Has a Kryptonite

5. **He has weak Points:** Every man has clay feet. What is a clay foot? An area of deficiency; an inadequacy. Something he is not very proud of. A secret addiction. A thumbscrew. A gap in a castle wall. A reason for insecurity, an uncontrollable emotion. A need. Sometimes it's a small, secret pleasure. A shameful act. A secret life. Something he is most vulnerable to. If you have seen any of the Superman movies, you will learn something exciting about the Man of Steel. First, you will see a dual picture of a meek and bumbling man, who everyone felt was no threat in Clark Kent, and in that same man lies Superman. On one hand, he is weak, powerless, and a nonentity, while on the other, Clark Kent transforms into Superman: **The man of steel.** Faster than a speeding bullet. Able to catch a falling plane in the sky and bring it to safety. The whole world loves and wants more of him. He rules the headlines and dictates every breaking news. Yet in all this incredible display of power, he has a weakness: *Kryptonite.* A powerful greenish kind of gem imported from faraway Krypton, his home planet. This object is capable of sapping Superman of all his abilities and rendering him ordinary. To deal with him, you must know his weakness and use it to control him.

Samson was a mighty man of power. With his bare arms he tore a lion into two and used the jaw bone of an ass to destroy 1000 Philistines. He was a one-man army that no man could tame. But he had a weakness. His hair. If that were to be cut, he would lose all his strength and be like any other man. **Judges 16:17.** Goliath's weakness was his unprotected forehead. All David needed to do was to send the stone right into the middle of his forehead. Every great man has an unprotected forehead. Every Achilles has an unprotected heel. Achilles was a mythical Greek hero of the Iliad. A foremost Greek warrior at the siege of Troy. When he was a baby, his mother tried to make him immortal by bathing him in a magical river, but the heel by which she held him remained vulnerable…his Achilles heel. No matter how together, organized, and put-together a man appears to you, there is a part of him where he does not have it together. To the Apostle Paul, it was his thorn in the flesh. Most of the time, when we say people cannot be tempted, we are referring to individuals who have not been tempted in their areas of weakness. They appear larger than life as they walk through temptation, without a scar or a stain.

To many, they are people of the highest moral standards. But that is not entirely (always) true. What they don't tell you is that they were simply tempted in their area of strength. Not in their area of weakness. For example, a man whom women cannot tempt can be tempted by money or some other "Kryptonite". Only Jesus was tempted at all points and came out without sin. **Hebrews 4:15.** God is so good that He does not allow us to be tempted at all points. He orchestrates the temptation in such a way that only the ones we can overcome are allowed to come to us. The ones we can't handle, he keeps away from us. ***A strong man is one whose weakness is unknown.*** To catch a man and keep him for life, you must seek to find his kryptonite, his weak point and make yourself a cure. An antidote; a poison killer. Once he sees you as the one who covers his weakness, he will hold onto you for life.

You ask, "But how can I know his weak point?" Simple, you must create an environment that allows him to open up to you. You must detach yourself emotionally from him so that you can see him objectively. Allow him to be himself in your presence. Avoid judgmental attitudes that cause him to run back into his shell and hide. Create an atmosphere of trust and love. Unconditional love.

Be his mother without trying to control him. Let him go and let him return to you. Be supportive and let him know you love him, despite his shortcomings. Don't just say it, prove it, be his friend, his confidant. Be patient with him. Very patient.

Above all, open up to him about your secrets. *Deep calleth deep.* Win his trust by unveiling yourself to him. Make him think he has something on you. No man finds it easy to walk out on a woman who truly knows him. Never succumb to the temptation to use the information he has given you about himself against him. No matter the situation, show him that you can be loyal, regardless of how it works out between the two of you. He may walk out on you, but he will never get over you. Most times, such men come back because they can't find such loyalty anywhere else.

Let's move on.

HE IS INFLUENCED BY PEOPLE HE TRUSTS

He can be influenced by those he trusts: the word "influence" is very powerful. It means to act upon. To have and exert influence or effect. To work on. To claim, tempt, or induce into action by using one's charm. It also means to determine, shape, mold, and regulate. To give direction. It does not mean taking over and driving; it is directing the driver's path. It is usually a passive thing. People who influence are generally not seen. They prefer to stay in the background and pull the strings from there.

Influence is also the effect a person has on another. A man can be influenced by his mother to be whatever the dominant mother chooses him to be. Whenever you see the Seat of power, look out for the Seat of influence. Usually, it is located very close to the seat of power. A man may occupy the seat of power in his house. He is the ruler, and he makes decisions for everyone. However, you may find that another family member, such as his wife or one of the children, influences the decisions he makes. In some queer situations, it is the house help or servant that controls and influences the whole house! When you fail to recognize this power dynamic and disregard its influence, you end up falling out of favor with everyone else and not understand why. To know a man, you must study what influences him. If you ignore those influences, you will start well with him and later find that the two of you have become pawns in someone's chessboard. Before you met him, there were people already in his life; don't underrate their influence, use it to your advantage.

Men can be significantly influenced by people they trust. People who have, over time, proven in words and deeds that they have their interest at heart. Look out for such people. People in his life who have to "approve" of you before he goes on dating you. (Not that their approval should matter if you both love each other.) You may not be aware of such discussions about you. Who are these people? They exist within the circle of his life.

For Example, His Parents: To win the man is to win the heart of his parent or parents. If he has a mother and they are very close, you must not seek to present yourself as an alternative to his relationship with his mother. Don't see her as a rival you must fight and break him from. You will fail woefully. A man will easily lose a wife than a mother. He reasons that a wife, or a lover (fiancée), he can replace, but not a mother. Realize this and be wise. In choosing battles, it is wise to choose which battles to fight and which to avoid. Don't compete with influence, work with it. To get a man to trust you so that you can influence him, you must be seen to love those who are already in his life. Offend them and you may lose out. Focus your attention on winning the trust and love of those who are influencing him. His parents. His siblings. His friends. His Boss. His Pastor. His Role model. Find the people he keeps talking about and get to know them. Once you win their hearts, you have secured your place in their lives. Even when trouble comes in the future between the two of you, they will stand up for you and fight for you.

Women sometimes make this grave mistake. They think "oh it's just the two of us and nobody else….." nothing could be more erroneous. To control the king, you must control the people controlling him. You have a job to do. Now you've gotten him, get those who have him. Go out of your way to be nice to them. Win them. If you ignore them, they will see you as an intruder who wants to take their place in the man's heart. Avoid unnecessary rivalry. The fewer enemies you have, the better for you.

Once you've gotten them on your side, you have bought enough time to establish yourself fully in his life. Soon, you become the dominant influence in his life. One he can trust. The keyword here is "Trust." Can he trust you? Are you worthy of trust? Do you think, knowing all that you know of yourself, you deserve to be trusted? Would you trust yourself? If your answer to these questions is yes, then people will trust you. Don't try to get people out of his life because you feel they are not suitable for him. Not when your place is not yet sure. Restrain yourself from criticizing people he loves and respects. Wait for your time. Don't give your opinion when it has not been sought. Keep it to yourself. Write it somewhere, maybe in your journal or diary. Observe and learn. What is it about them that makes him feel the way he does about them? Even when he makes a negative comment about them to you, expecting you to agree with it and even take it further, resist the temptation and keep quiet or offer an excuse for their behavior.

Feelings are traitors. Never to be trusted. It changes like the weather. Never let it deceive you. For example, He makes a negative remark about his mother, probably because he is angry at that moment. Don't ever support it. Defend her or keep quiet. Win his trust by not attacking those he trusts. Until then, wait for your time. Trust takes time to build. He may love you and still not trust you. "I love you" and "I trust you" do not sound alike to me. Does it sound the same to you? I guess not. With time, patience, and wisdom, love evolves into trust, which in turn gives way to influence.

Influence means you are calling the shots. If you love him, you must love the people who love him. Please don't ignore them, nor try to take him away from them.

This study aims to provide a clear and concise understanding of how men perceive themselves and their inner nature. I have also taken the time to point out the problems and, at the same time, proffer solutions to them. One person may not exhibit all these features simultaneously. However, we aim to prepare you for whatever situation you may encounter. The only way to avoid being a victim of life is to seek and acquire wisdom. That is why I believe you are reading this book at this moment.

7. **He is Ambitious:** How do you handle an ambitious man? First, what does it mean to be ambitious? It means to have a strong desire for success or achievement. Ambition means a cherished desire. An ambition, a dream. It is a strong drive that propels a man to success. Every man has an ambition. Something he is trying to be or achieve. A goal. A driving desire. Sometimes, some men don't express it, while others do. Even the most harmless-looking person you know has an ambition. Some negative, some positive. Adolph Hitler. The German Nazi

dictator who killed over 6 million Jews in his bid to exterminate the entire Jewish nation from the face of the earth. He had an ambition. A diabolic and satanic one. It was his dream to have a world free from Jewish "pollution," as he called it. He failed.

Henry Ford, the founder of Ford Motor Company, had an ambitious goal: to put a Ford car in every American home. Today, that dream has come to pass. He pioneered the mass production of automobiles as we have them today.

Martin Luther King had an ambition. He dreamed that one day all people, regardless of their skin color, would be judged by the content of their character. He dreamed of a day when all black and white would live together in harmony as one, equal in the eyes of God. That dream is becoming a reality every day in the United States. Racial discrimination is a significant offence in that country today. It was not so then. Every man has an ambition. To one, it may be to marry a beautiful wife and raise beautiful children. Another may be to build a house in his father's compound. To another, it may be to be enormously wealthy, while his neighbor wants to have enough to get by. As our faces are different, so are our ambitions. To catch a man, you must identify what is driving him. You must know what his dreams are. If his ambition is not in agreement with yours, you will have a problem with him. **"Can two walk together if they do not agree?" Amos 3:3**

If you don't know his ambition, you don't know him. You cannot master what you don't know.

What does he talk about?

What does he respond to?

What is he emotional about?

Knowing your man is understanding what has his attention and helping him to achieve it. Men don't take it lightly with those who trifle with their ambitions. If you make a joke of it or mock it, you may be committing an unpardonable sin. Tread wisely. Be a listening ear: a supportive voice and a helping hand.

8. **He Hates Commitment:** This is not a very complimentary thing to say about my gender, but it is the truth. Men hate commitment. They get scared when they think someone is trying to catch them and keep them. Asking him to commit to you may not be the best idea at first.

First, what is commitment? It means to give something in trust to another. It talks about total devotion. Telling a man to commit himself to you is no smarter than it is to demand that a fish bite your hook. Fish don't go biting a hook! They bite baits. Please don't get so desperate about catching and keeping him that it shows up in your behavior. Once the fish sees it is a trap, it will flee. Yes, he wants you to be his, but he doesn't want to be yours. It's wild isn't it? Yes, he knows he is yours, but don't rub it in, especially when he has not put a ring on your finger. Girls often make mistakes in this area. Some ladies, in a bid to win the man, move into his house and put their pictures and portraits all over the place. Do crazy things like telling everyone to clear off? Baby girl, that is wrong! So wrong. Don't scare him. Guys freak out when they feel someone is trying to own them. Let that happen on the wedding day. Take only the place he gives you. Please don't go into his room when he hasn't invited you. Don't even go to visit him unless he begs you to. Give him the impression that you are not crazy about him. That is what drives him crazy. Make him look for you by knowing when to be scarce. Don't always take his phone calls, especially when he calls at odd hours. Decline invitations and even refuse certain gifts he offers you. No matter what he does or says, keep your distance. Don't go about telling people "he is my husband" when he has yet to see your parents!

What are you? Crazy? Stop! Take a deep breath and ease off. Take a vacation. Do something else. Get him off your mind. Some ladies make the mistake of even demanding that he come and meet their parents or get married to them when he isn't ready yet. It's not for you to decide that. If you have played your cards well and have won his affections and respect, he will do what he knows he wants to do. Yes, I know you love him and want him so much. Control yourself, girl! Think. To catch a prey, you must not be seen by the prey. Hide your true intentions and let him take the initiative. In the chapter "Laws of Seduction," I will show you how to make him commit to you without asking him to do so.

9. **He hates Responsibility:** This is another sad comment to make about my brothers. But this is the truth. Forget about the picture you grew up with of your knight in shining armor. That knight never made it. Again, what is Responsibility? It is a form of trustworthiness—the traits of being answerable to someone for something or being responsible for one's conduct. John D. Rockefeller Jnr once said, "We must instill a sense of duty in our children. Every right implies a responsibility, every opportunity, an obligation, every possession a duty." Another wise man once said, *with great power comes great responsibility.*" Winston Churchill adds, "Responsibility is the price for greatness."

Responsibility is a necessary virtue, albeit a hated but necessary virtue. People are constantly working to escape responsibility. We would love to eat our cake and have it. And when we can't have it, we throw a fit. Responsibility is not natural. It is acquired. It is the necessary thorny road all men must walk to attain greatness in life and the hereafter. In seeking a relationship with the man of your life, bear this in mind. He is not looking for another responsibility; he is looking for a helper. One who will make life easier for him. Yes, he knows what he should do, but you must have a way of getting him to do it without seeming like another problem in his life. Some women erroneously view a relationship as a form of economic relief. They see men as burden bearers. One who will come to carry away all their problems. He is not looking for more problems; he is looking for a life partner. A companion and confidant. A burden sharer.

Men get scared when women become too demanding on them. Some ladies go so far as to share all their family problems with him: Their father's unpaid pension, their accumulating rents. Unpaid school fees for family members. Soon, they turn the man into a welfare industry that keeps churning out resources. This is wrong. Don't let him see you as another liability. Before you even qualify to be in a relationship, you must achieve a level of self-reliance. Get a job. Learn a trade. Do something with yourself. Go to school to acquire a skill. Get busy. Don't see him as a ticket to escape poverty.

Escape poverty before he shows up in your life. Don't turn every meeting into another asking spree. Soon, he begins to dread your phone calls or your presence. Next, he will start to avoid you. Avoid this. Even when he pretends he doesn't mind paying your bills, don't be deceived, he minds. Don't always look for what he will give you; look for what you can give him. I am not saying he shouldn't give you gifts or do things for you. He should. That's what it takes to be a man. But don't overdo it. When he offers to do something for you or give you something, when you refuse, does he insist? Does he take offence? If so, then let him; if not, avoid it. I know you have problems. We all do.

To catch a man and keep him for life, you must do your best not to make yourself another of his problems. You are worth much more than that. Put your faith in God, and He will take care of you. Only God can say, **"Cast all your cares on me, for I care for you". 1 Peter 5:7.** Learn how to channel your cares to God, and He will make a way for you. Don't turn a man into your God. One, you may lose him eventually, and two, God will turn His back on you. Put your trust in God. He will help you. Nothing humbles a man like a woman whose trust is not in him but in God. It puts him in a position where he struggles to find relevance in her life. Especially when he knows and sees how God helps her through other sources. Responsibility is a threat to romance. Do you want to keep him for life? Then don't take him. Ignore his assets. Pretend not to notice it. Don't appear taken by the display of his wealth. Ignore them. Let him know it is not his possessions you are after, it is him you want. If you have him, you will still possess his possessions. Be wise, my sister.

I hope this information is helpful to someone.

10. **He hates Competition:** Nobody enjoys being second. Everyone wants to be first and only. To catch a man and keep him for life, you must understand how to use this knowledge wisely. The word competition means to have another contender. It is the process of trying to beat others. The process of trying to win and do better than others. The word competition suggests other words like:

Contest: an activity in which people try to win something or do better than others.

Opposition: the rival, with whom we compete.

Struggle: a contest between factions over a limited source.

Men like to think they are special, that there is no one like them. That the whole world revolves around their little finger. They can be delusional. They imagine they are the only ones who see what they see in a woman. Competition can come in handy. If you want him to desire you more, create a sense of competition. Let him know he is not the only eligible bachelor in town. This is not to suggest that you cheat or double date, far from it. Men want what everyone else wants. They feel a sense of accomplishment when they eventually get it. The price of a prey is determined by who it was taken from. If nobody wants it, nobody wants it. One way to put him on edge is to talk about other people like him whom you admire. Do it so innocently that he will do everything to outdo that perceived rival. Don't compare him with someone else; this can be counterproductive. Just let him know he is one of your potential contenders. How do you feel when you go to the market and you see something you love and want to own? How do you think when the seller tells you that someone is coming to pay for it tomorrow, and it's the only one in the market? You will immediately commit to it by paying an installment or paying cash and collecting it. Competition creates value. Men want to know that if they don't get you, someone else will. It puts pressure on him to act fast.

Instead of asking him to marry you, tell him about the many suitors "disturbing" you for your hand in marriage. Pretend to ask him for counsel on whom to agree to. This is assuming you are just dating and he has not made any moves. To put him under pressure – men tend to perform better under pressure – create a competitive environment. Ask him to help you pray for clarity. If he is genuinely interested in you, he will act fast. Just knowing that someone else wants what you're trying to get and is even willing to offer a higher price makes you want to rush for it. But if you feel that no one wants it, you won't be in a hurry to take it. Men often dislike competition, yet they usually thrive in it. A woman who knows how to use this weapon does not need to act desperate. Let him know that you are not entirely his until he weds you properly in the church or in a place that aligns with your faith. Until then, the competition continues. Keep him on his toes. Keep him working to gain your favor. Make him work hard to earn your affection; that is the only way he will treat you with value. People tend to value what they fight to get. Make it too easy for him, and he will despise it.

11. **He Hates Confrontation:** A confrontation is simply a bold challenge, a discord resulting from a clash of ideas or opinions. A face-off. A showdown. An encounter, a hostile disagreement on a face-to-face level. In all relationships, conflicts and discord are inevitable. There is no perfect relationship. As long as two people or more are involved, with their differing perspectives and values, there will inevitably be seasons of disagreement. To win a man, you must avoid confrontations. It is not a confrontation until two or more people are involved. Rule your emotions to the point that you can't be offended by him. Smile when they expect you to blow your top. Avoid that temptation to give him a piece of your mind. Nothing ruins a person's good name like when they have a reputation of being confrontational and quarrelsome. Seek the path of diplomacy and depend on God in prayer. Man is designed in such a way that something in him responds to a woman who does not show him respect. I understand it can be difficult to remain silent and endure the verbal abuse. However, this is often the best way to manage a situation that could escalate, especially

when your safety is at stake.. Do not get into a shouting match with him, just walk away. Your mental is your number one priority. Are you in a relationship with a man who abuses you both verbally and physically? Simply walk out of it. Do it gracefully. Don't take the law into your own hands. He has not committed to marrying you, yet he continues to treat you with indifference and disrespect. What leads you to believe that his behavior will magically change after you tie the knot? It's time to wake up to the reality of your situation! You need to empower yourself with the knowledge and strength to end a relationship that is unhealthy and unfulfilling. Maintain your calm and take action. But if you must remain in that relationship, then you must adopt wisdom.

Do this:

I. Avoid those matters that lead to quarrels. If he is insisting on his point of view, pull back and leave the matter there.

ii. Learn to say "I am sorry". It works like magic. It is the water that quenches all the fires of emotions and hurt. A simple three-worded statement can sink a shipload of tension. "I am sorry."

iii. Study his moods and know the best time to present your case. Do it in a non- confrontational way.

iv. Observe the principle of submission and yieldedness. Don't be stiff and unbending; a little compromise sometimes won't hurt. When I say compromise, I mean on non–harmful matters that don't revolve around life and faith.

"A soft word" the bible says "breaks the bone". It breaks resistance and stubbornness. Stubbornness cannot handle softness Proverbs 25:15. A soft answer can turn away wrath.

Proverbs 15:1. It can deflate the most unfriendly countenance. Use it. Why did David marry Abigail, the former wife of Nabal? Her tongue. She knew how to speak to him (1 Samuel 25:32–33). That your voice is the loudest and your argument is the strongest can mean nothing else than that your influence is waning—change strategy.

12. He gets bored easily: Men get bored easily. You may not know it at first glance. They are quick to lose interest in something they once found enjoyable. What does it mean to be bored? It means to be world-weary. Tired of the world. It means uninterested because of frequent exposure or indulgence. It is the phase a person enters when they have achieved their life goal. Success can bring boredom, but as long as you still have something you haven't acquired, you maintain enthusiasm. Boredom is dangerous. It leads to terrible habits like depression. It comes out of a routine, constant exposure to the same thing. Soon, we lose that sense of hunger and appeal. Ordinary creates boredom. Routine creates boredom. Accomplishment not improved upon creates boredom. How do you deal with a man who tends to get bored easily? Can you help it if he gets bored with you? Are there secrets to apply to stop this from happening? What gets a man bored with a woman? Why does he seem so interested at the beginning and suddenly lose interest after a while? You hear girls complaining, "you don't call like you used to call before," and the guy has a lot of good reasons to give. What does it take to keep the fire of his passion burning for you? How do you prevent him from getting too comfortable with you?

The major reason men get bored easily is the failure of expectations. They expect too much out of a relationship and eventually think they are not getting everything they thought they would get. They have this funny idea from one bloated, overrated fantasy about women. I would say that those failed expectations are actually overrated. Ridiculous, to say the least. They have this crazy picture in their mind of what is not real and feel disappointed when it turns out not to be so. Another reason men get bored easily is overindulgence. People tend to get too familiar with something they have easy access to. While trying to build a lasting relationship with the man of your dreams, try not always to be available to him. Learn the secret art of scarcity. Economics tells us that once a product is scarce in the market, its value or cost will skyrocket. But once it overflows the market, the value drops. Too much of everything is not good. Don't give him full access to your entire self. Don't bombard him with too much affection. Affection is good—a vital ingredient for lasting love. However, too much of it can be fatal. Even the Bible warns us to withdraw our feet from our neighbor's house **"lest he be weary of thee and so hate thee" Prov: 25:17.** It is good to show friendliness, but it can destroy a relationship when it is not used wisely.

Another reason men get bored easily is pre-marital sex. Sex is good, but should be reserved only for marriage. This is not just a religious or Christian injunction; it is wisdom. Why give out all your goods to someone who hasn't paid for them? Only for him to eat and dump it for another because he has no commitment to you? Be wise, my beloved sister. Men are hunters. All they want to do is to conquer you and add you to their list of acquired territories. No man who wants a permanent relationship with a woman he loves talks about sex before marriage. Don't fall for the "if you love me, you will give it to me" trap.. It's a trick to play on your emotions; it makes you feel guilty for not obliging him and blackmails you into a position of compromise. Soon, you pay the price of heartbreak. Don't let it happen to you. If you want to keep this man, don't give him everything he wants till he takes you to the altar. This is the truth. If he really loves you, he will respect your decision for chastity and will cooperate with you, knowing you can be trusted. You see, the problem with consenting to sex before marriage is that once you do it with that man, he imagines it must be how you give in to other men. Consequently, he loses respect for you and ditches you. Some deluded people reason that, to keep him, give him sex. Nothing could be farther from the truth. The opposite is what happens. You lose his trust and respect, and he begins to see you as a cheap, easy lay, and soon walks away. This is the truth. When you keep your chastity, you keep your man. You earn respect, trust, and unending love. Apart from contracting sexually transmitted diseases that can be detrimental to your health, you may get pregnant and instantly become a problem that he wants to run away from. Be wise. I know you are wise. Let's go into other things you must know about men.

13 **He loves to have the Upper hand**: Man is a born competitor. He is always scheming to take over. To move ahead of others. To gain power and control. It is inborn. To catch a man and keep him for life, you will have to deal with this fact. What does it mean to have the upper hand? It means to have a position of advantage and control. To catch a man, you must know how to position yourself in such a way that makes him feel he has an upper hand in the affair. Concede to him in all matters. Treat him like a king. Boost his ego. Point out those positive things you see in him and like. Let him feel secure in knowing that his authority will not be challenged or undermined. Men often have ego deficiencies that require treatment by a discerning and understanding woman. Learn to feed that need for affirmation and acceptance. Make him Lord and Master but wisely decline

from whatever he demands that does not agree with your principle or faith. But do it gracefully. Use your womanhood. You can make a man agree to whatever you say if you know how to be a true woman. Give him the upper hand, and soon he will be feeding from your palms.

14. He loves gain without effort: The less effort it takes to get something, the better it is. Who wants to expend unnecessary energy on fruitless pursuits? Men love it to be easy and cheap. To achieve more results with minimal effort, you need superior strategies. You also need great contacts—people who can help you get where you are going quicker. Man is basically a lazy creature, most times. He loves life on a platter of gold. He loves luxury. To keep a man, you must evolve a structure that makes him feel good about expending effort, without feeling that he is doing much. Look at what he is doing or pursuing and find ways you can help him achieve his goals without having to do so much. You can become his counselor. His helper. As men, we tend to become attached to what makes life easier for us. Get him hooked on you by helping him achieve more with minimal effort.

15. He loves taking credit even for doing nothing: Don't get offended about this trait when you see it in some men. That is the way some men are. While some men expend themselves to invent new ideas and products, others simply want to stand by and reap the benefits of the inventor's work, claiming credit for the job. We see this in the brazen rape of creativity and ideas being suffered by people of the arts. Pirates want to let you do all the work while they dive in to reap where they did not sow. This is a negative human tendency. It is selfish and wicked. People want others to do all the dirty work while they take the credit. Don't let this happen to you. Don't be used.

HE HAS A TENDENCY TO FLIRT AND CHEAT

16.   He tends to flirt: What is Flirting? Are all men flirts? Is it possible for a man to love only one woman? Should we accept flirting as a normal part of a man's behavior, or should we confront it and work against it? Whatever way you choose to look at it, flirting and infidelity are problem that exists in our world today. Not just men, but women also flirt. But not all women. It seems to me like the world is divided into two types of people – those who flirt and those who fight the temptation to flirt.

First of all, what is flirting? It simply means to talk or behave amorously without serious intentions; It means to toy with people's emotions and affections; To arouse one's sexuality. It's like a seductive woman who uses her sex appeal to exploit men. Flirting is any playful behavior intended to arouse sexual interest.

What's the difference between flirting and cheating?

"Flirting and cheating differ in their intent and impact on a relationship. Flirting is playful, lighthearted, and often harmless, expressing interest without the intention of causing harm. Cheating, on the other hand, involves a deliberate betrayal of trust and intimacy with a partner, often involving emotional or physical intimacy with someone outside the relationship" Wikipedia

Are all men flirts? Hardly. Some good men believe in honoring and preserving the sanctity and dignity of the opposite sex. Real men. But these men are in terribly short supply. The majority are nothing but sexual predators seeking whom they may devour. They start as nice, promising prospects with words filled with promises and hopes. All the while, they are hunters laying a snare for prey. Be warned. What they say to you, they say to others like you. Words that they hope you will believe, and by doing so, let down your defenses.

How to identify a flirting man:

i. Are his words sweet and too good to be true?

ii) Does he deliberately sweep you off your feet with his charm?

iii. Does he use flattering words to describe you to the extent that you wonder whether they are true?

iv. Is he too good to be single?

v. Does he appear vague and closed up when discussing his past experiences?

vi. Are his stories inconsistent?

vii. Does he seem too experienced in the way he takes you off your feet?

viii. Does he bombard you with gifts?

ix.   Does he make premature gestures of intimate advances towards you?

x. Does he seem to be in a hurry?

xi. Do you seem to be getting a lot of bad reports about his former relationships?

xii. Does he seem to be in a hurry to have sex with you, under the guise that "after all, we are getting married"? Does he touch you inappropriately?

xiii. Does he seem to want to get you into a state of emotional blackmail, almost trying hard to make you love him?

Beware of such men. You could be dealing with a Casanova. A flirt, a cheat. All he will do is take your love, use it, and discard it. You mean nothing to him. Now, some men who flirt do so because they do not know better. They are simply doing what their friends do or what people in their environment do. They are not chronic flirts. Such men are curable. Once they find a true woman who won't fall for those charms, they will give up and change. But in the general analysis, every man has at one point toyed with the thought, at least the thought of cheating. The difference is that some wave it off as a stupid idea and move on, while others allow these thoughts to take hold of them until they become actions, and soon, actions become a habit, and ultimately, a habit becomes a character.

Are you dating a man who you suspect has flirting tendencies that can be cured? Do you need help?

(i) If the relationship has not gone far, as in marriage, it may be wise to let him go now. If his eyes seem to be elsewhere, you will do well to let him go.

(ii) Don't be too trusting. Investigate everything he says. Ask around. Do your espionage work on him. Take note of what he says and hold him accountable to them. Let him know you are not a fool. Men generally flirt or cheat because of the trust their partners bestow on them.

(iii) Set standards for him. Let him know his actions will have consequences: losing you. If he thinks he can get away with it, like he did the last time, he will do it again. Make it very tough for him. Even when you choose to forgive him, let him pay dearly for it. He won't try it again.

Note: A man can be in love with his woman and still cheat on her. Love is not the issue. To some men, it's just a game. A pastime. A way of releasing tension and pressure. The key is to let him know that this form of behavior won't be accepted.

(iv) Study the mind of a flirting and cheating man. If you understand how they think, you can anticipate their next move and prevent it. Once he realizes that he can't keep doing this without getting into trouble with you, he will stop. Remember, he is not doing this because he hates you. It's not always about you; it's about him. It's a bad habit you can help him break. To catch him and keep him for life, you must learn how to contain the flirt in him. It is often better not to continue a relationship with this type of man if you have not gone too far or gotten married. Better a broken engagement than a broken marriage. If he cheats on you now that you are not married, what is the guarantee he won't do worse after you are married? Of course, there is always room for pardon; every man deserves a second chance, that is, if he is willing to change. However, if you notice a repetition of this behavior, it would be wise to call it off.

(v) Demand of him to submit to a monitoring authority. A Pastor, a respected leader. Someone he respects. If he knows that someone like that might hear about his indiscretions, he won't fall into it again. He must be subject to something or someone. He must submit himself to an accountability structure.

(vi) Ask him to give you full access to all his devices, including passwords and passcodes for his phones, tablets, laptop, desktop, etc. A man who wants to be trusted again has nothing to hide. If he refuses to give you such access, he is not yet ready to change his ways. Don't believe a word he says.

In the next session, I will tell you the types of men you do not want to catch. Men who can ruin your life.

Reasons some men cheat

i. Because they think they can

ii. They feel they are too much for one woman to keep.

iii. They are not content with who God gave them.

iv. Boredom

v. Failed expectations from their partner. She did not turn out to be what he thought she was.

vi. Bad company. If his friends flirt and cheat, they provide him with a friendly environment to carry out his cheating tendencies. If, on the other hand, he has good people around him, who value the integrity of their union and never flirt or cheat, he too will find a reason to change. **"Evil communications corrupt good manners" 1 Corinthians 15:33**

vii. They cheat because the opportunity presented itself. Too much opportunity creates too much temptation. Opportunity is the greatest seduction. Don't take unnecessary risks with your man. For example, please don't ask your female best friend to come and take care of him while you are away. That is like going to the devil's door and knocking and wondering why he answers. A man should not be allowed to be alone with the opposite sex if he has shown such tendencies before. Most times, they fall not because they want to flirt, but because temptation comes calling in the form of an opportunity and unwisely trusting him with a female.

viii. Another reason they cheat is that they don't have a strong commitment to God. They don't have a living and active relationship with God. Be careful how you get intimate with a man who is not intimate with God. Sometimes it takes the influence of God in him to say "No" to temptation. If he fears God, that can keep him from cheating. Pray for a man who fears God. And if you are already involved with someone who doesn't know God, start praying for their salvation. With prayer, God can save the so-called "irredeemable".

ix. Some men cheat because of bad leadership given by those they looked up to. Sometimes it could be from their father. Or a person they considered an example worthy of emulation. For example, the Monica Lewinsky/Bill Clinton scandal served to establish a new paradigm of leadership failure and moral indiscretion in high places. If the leader, who is supposed to be flawless and above board, can stoop so low and still get away with it, what stops people of a lesser class from doing the same, or even worse? A man needs a model. Someone who has modeled faithfulness, fidelity, and honor in his relationship with his spouse. One example can be enough to save a generation. So when he cheats, he does so with a sense of justification and vindication – "after all," he reasons, "I am not the only one" It's almost as if the unspoken mantra in our confused world is "Everybody is doing it, so it can't be wrong". God help us!

x. Another reason a man may cheat is that he is not in love with the person he is with. It is possible that, through some twist of fate, the relationship came to be. A man may even marry a woman not because he loves her but because he pities her. He tells himself, "If I don't marry her, who will?" Or, "I have already promised her marriage, I must marry her even though I know I don't love her." Soon, he realizes his mistake and feels stuck. As a way of getting away from the real world, he seeks love elsewhere. He is married to "Leah," but his heart belongs to "Rachael." Such a man, no matter what you do to please him, will never love you. The whole thing was not meant to be that way. It was a mistake. What must a woman do in this case? Let him go and fast. Don't allow a man to marry you because of sentiments, as they soon fade away, and he begins to regret his actions. If he does not love you, do both of you a favor and let him go before it is too late.

In one section, I show you how to know a man is in love with you. Additionally, I will show you how to recognize when he is through with you.

HE IS ALWAYS SEARCHING

17. **He is constantly searching**: Man is always searching. There is always something out there that attracts his curiosity. He searches for answers to questions that no one seems to have. Questions about his existence. How he came into the earth. The mystery behind his purpose. Why was he born into the family he was born into? Questions about his identity, who he is, and why he is the way he is. Questions about his personality and how others perceive him. Questions about God. Is there a God? Is there a supreme being out there running the universe? Who is He and what does He want from him? Is there life after death, and if so, where will his soul appear after death?

Questions, questions, questions. Questions about the opposite sex. Why are women so different? So unique? So complex? He is searching for answers. If you want to know your man, you must be aware of the object of his search. He is searching for someone who will love him as he is. Someone who has the answer to his search. He is searching for you. Are you the one he is searching for, or must he seek another? He is also searching for fantasy. Somehow, in his mind, he has a picture of a love that is not. He lives with the unreal woman in his heart. He is married to her and to whoever falls into her image. This is why he goes from one relationship to another. He is searching for someone who doesn't exist, yet he believes he will find her. Who is she? Does she exist somewhere? Maybe in another dimension? Where did he first see her? On a picture or the television screen? Or in the fleeting encounter with a strange woman during a lift or a taxi ride? What he does not realize is that the picture he saw of her was a short, incomplete frame of a not-too-perfect personality magnified within that small window of time and chance. He saw a bit of her and now fantasizes about an unreal, inaccurate, misleading picture of a person he hardly knows. And bases his judgment of his true (real life) love on that fantasy image, and if this true love does not meet up with this image in his mind of a woman he never really knew, he falls out of love with her. Some men fantasize a lot, and fantasies should be treated with the same attention they deserve, not to be brought into the real world. He is always thinking of someone. He imagines that things are as they seem, but when he gets close, he finds something else. Ensure your man is not still living in a world of fantasies. If so, he needs a reality check. He needs to wake up to what is. He needs to realize that there is no perfect woman who possesses everything he will ever require. He needs to learn not to seek happiness in what he does not have, but to learn to be happy with what he has. (I hope he is reading this.) To catch a man, bring up this issue with him and let him open up to you. Fantasies die when they meet with reality.

Just as a fisherman selects his catch, you, too, have the power to choose the right man for you. Not every man is worth your time and affection. If you find that you've caught the wrong fish, don't hesitate to release it back into the sea. You can decide who is worthy of your love and who is not.

In this section, we will discuss types of men to catch and men not to catch or dump when caught mistakenly. I will also show you the signs you must look for to end a bad relationship. There is nothing that gives a woman more power in a relationship than the ability to end it herself. It is better to call it off by yourself than to wait to be dumped like a piece of rag. Once a man begins to show signs that he is getting tired of you, dump him. Do it before he does it. In the next chapter, I will show you how to know when he is through with you and how to hit before he does. You see, a woman who can dump a man is a superwoman. That demonstration that you are not desperate about him and that you can do fine without him is all he needs to be humble and subdued. Next time he gets into a relationship, he will handle that next person with care. By this you would have helped someone else. But first, let's see the types of men you don't want in your life.

MEN YOU DO NOT WANT TO CATCH

Chapter Three

15 MEN YOU DO NOT WANT TO CATCH

In your quest for the right man to catch here are the toxic men you should run away from.

1. **Mr. Sweet Mouth**

Have you met people who seem to know what others will like to hear and say it to them? Be careful with such. They flatter with their mouths to lay a trap for their unsuspecting victims. They know what you like to hear, and they say it to seduce you so that they can take advantage of you. Most of the time, their claims are never fact-checked. They exaggerate a lot to make it sweet and nice. They tell you how beautiful you are, even when they think you aren't that much (pardon my sarcasm). They call you pet names and make lofty promises they can't keep. If you are the type who laps up words of affirmation, if you suffer from low self-esteem and need to hear people say nice things to you, you will most likely fall victim to such men. They seem to choose their victims. They know who needs sweet words.

To escape such men, rebuild your self-esteem by developing a strong relationship with God and with yourself. If you don't accept and celebrate yourself for who you are, no one will. Don't fall victim to those sweet mouths who want only one thing from you – sex, and once they get it, they are gone. These are not the type you want to catch unless you are like them. Then you don't need this book! This does not suggest that good men won't speak sweet words to you. The difference is that they say it to build you up and not to take advantage of you. As a rule, never follow what people say to you; watch what they do. A man is what he does. He can say anything to hide his true intentions. Be cautious.

2. Mr. Angry

"Make no friendship with an angry man, and with a furious man thou shall not go" Proverbs 22:24. Anger is a natural human emotion. It has its place. Anger on its own is not evil. It can be used to accomplish just and noble causes. Anger is defined as a strong emotion. A feeling that is oriented towards some real or supposed grievance. It is belligerence aroused by a real or imagined wrong. We all get angry, and sometimes justly so.

Even God gets angry. Moses was not allowed to enter the Promised Land because God was angry with him. "The Lord was angry with me for your sakes and said, ' You shall not enter Canaan with me also" Deuteronomy 1:37. Psalm 7:11 states that "God is angry with the sinner every day." Anger cannot be a sin, or God would be a sinner. Paul admonishing us about anger counseled, "Be angry but sin not." He even adds, "Let not the sun go down upon your wrath (or anger)," Ephesians 4:26. So, there is a significant difference between being angry for a just cause and sinning or committing an offense through anger. Anger is not an excuse for breaking the law. When I say "Mr. Angry", I mean one who has no control over his emotions. One who is used by anger to destroy and damage.

Why must we rule over anger? Paul tells us in the next verse Ephesians 4:27 ***"Neither give place to the devil."*** That is to say, "Leave no such room or foothold for the devil (give no opportunity to him)." Amplified version. Uncontrolled anger gives the devil easy access into a man or woman's life to cause havoc". Such people have been known to go to unbelievable extremes. Some can kill or maim in one angry burst. Satan uses angry people. Before they know it, they have caused irreparable harm. You don't need such people in your life. How do you know Mr. Angry?

a. Does he easily get provoked?

b. Does he lightly raise his hand to strike?

c. Is he always involved in one contentious bout or another with other people?

d. Does he try to cut you off from people he is not on good terms with?

e. Does he say unprintable words of abuse to you or people when he is angry?

f. Does he scare you and make you uncomfortable?

G Does he show signs of abuse from others, like his parents? Does he come from an angry family?

H Is he the unforgiving type who seeks to avenge a past wrong?

Some of these characters may not be particularly bad, but others may be signs of trouble ahead. Example, Abuse. Whether verbal or physical. If he shows such signs, you must slow down and watch before committing.

3. **Mr. Mama's Boy**

Every person has a strong emotional bond with their parents. This is normal and healthy. In fact, a man who maltreats his mother will make life miserable for his wife. So on one end, we have the mama's boy, one who has an unusual attachment to his mother to the extent that she controls and manipulates him to do as she pleases. On the other end, we have the mama's nightmare – one who shows no regard for his mother. Insults her and sometimes physically abuses her. Run from them, especially when they tell you that they love you more than their mother. RUN! No man is supposed to love a woman more than his mother.

Because the love he has for his mother is a different type of love from the one he has for his wife, I can't love any other woman the way I love my wife. Neither can I love any other mother the way I love my mother. This is the way it should be. But the "mama's boy" is a problem. He is not suitable for a relationship. He can't seem to make decisions for himself, let alone make them for others. He is indecisive and controlled. Even when he breaks away from his mother, he will still need another mother figure to guide him. Mr. Mama's boy will break your heart. Everything you discuss with him will be discussed with "Mama" and he can't take a stand until she says so. So marrying him is also marrying his mother and being subject to that same manipulation. Soon, problem arises. If you can't change him, leave him to grow up. You don't have time to play baby sitter to a man who won't grow up. Life is too short.

MR ONE NIGHT STAND

4. Mr. One Night Stand

I call him "Mr. Hit and Run"! All he wants is sex. He does not love you, though he may say that. Love means nothing to him. To him, women are sex objects to be desired, handled, used, and dumped for another. They are cold and callous. They are hunters who go out to look for prey. They can't control their urge to explore new territories. If he has never had her before, he wants her. Once he has had her, he hates her. Watch how they immediately want to touch you and kiss you before taking you to the altar. He wants sex. He can even promise you marriage to get you to bed, and once you oblige him, he finds one excuse and calls off the engagement. Don't be a victim.

Keep your distance. Run from such. These types of men don't even feel any sense of remorse when they break a person's heart. To them, it's just a game. Lust is their motivation. Lust is not love. Lust is the desire to have, while love is the desire to give. They are not the same. However, lust can give, but his agenda is to take. It is still not the same as love. Love cares. Love is considerate. Love is not selfish. Love will not do anything to rob you of your dignity. Instead, it will protect and enhance it. Avoid "Mr. One Night Stand". If you are seeking a relationship that will last. Don't try to please him and give in to his sexual demands all in the bid to keep him – the opposite will happen, you will lose him and your self-dignity.

A man who has not mastered his sexual emotions is not fit to be in a relationship. Don't be another victim. Don't let someone add you to his list of options for his mood swings. He browses through his phone and wonders who he needs at the moment among a long list of other women. Suddenly, after breaking communication with you for a while, he seems to have remembered you. Why? You have made yourself one of the meals he can have at any time he wishes. So when he wants rice, he calls rice. When he needs beans, he calls for them, and when he wants to swallow, he calls for that too. Are you one of his lists of options, waiting for your turn to receive his attention? You are worth more than that! Are you in a relationship with Mr. One

Night Stand? Mr. Sex without marriage and commitment? Give him the boot now!

5. **Mr. People's Man**

What could be wrong with this type of man? Every man wants to be a people's man. There is nothing wrong with being liked by people. David was loved by people, so much that it got him into trouble with King Saul. There is a difference between being loved by people and being controlled by people. While people loved David, he was not necessarily controlled by them.

On the other hand, King Saul lost his place before God because he sought to be a man of the people. He placed people's wishes above the will of God for him. God fired him and replaced him with David, a man after His own heart. You need a man who will not be more disposed to what people tell him than to you. A man of the people cannot always be trusted. People control him. He listens to gossip, side talk, and hearsay. He would rather believe a gossip than believe you. He would rather take sides with people – friends, relatives, colleagues, neighbors than with you. Your secrets are not safe with him; soon, everybody will hear what you discussed in private. If you can't get him to break with the crowd and focus on you, you can't have him. Better let him go.

6. **Mr. Non-Verbal**

What does it mean to be non–verbal? To be verbal means to express your feelings in words. To speak. Whatever is expressed in spoken words. Everyone has feelings. The difference is in how we express it. Some use words; others follow up words with actions. A verbal person expresses himself in words. Therefore, a nonverbal person does not always express themselves in words. While such people may seem non–threatening, they can be very dangerous. Better a man who can express his anger or distaste in words, even when he has to scream and shout. Such people are easier to manage than those who appear calm but harbor anger. A non–verbal person is a mystery. They would stare at you blankly, only managing interjections of vague words and plastic expressions of friendship. You can't know them. The most reliable way to know a person is to listen to what they say. If you can't hear what they say, how can you possibly know them?

The solution to such men is to never assume with them. Never say you know them enough to take advantage of them. Don't mistake silence for weakness or consent. They may never have the courage to tell you that you have wronged them. They may prefer to tell it to another trusted friend or keep it to themselves. To manage such people, tread carefully. If you break a glass in his house, replace it with a new one. If you say or do something wrong to them, apologize even when they say they don't mind. Don't ever take him for granted. Don't assume, "Oh, he is a nice guy, he won't mind." You can be so wrong! He minds, it's just that he is not saying it. Such people tend to do something unexpected, such as ending a relationship or doing something unusual. If he is not talking or expressing emotions, use discretion, or if you are not the type to handle such people, walk away.

7. **Mr. Selfish Man**

All men are selfish. Selfishness is another effect of the fall of man. We want what pleases us. It's about us. Self-worship and love of self are not the same. Self–worship is narcissism. It is an exceptional and inordinate interest in and admiration for oneself. It shows up in feelings of excessive pride. It means conceit, vanity. This is where we derive selfishness.

On the other hand, loving oneself is simply doing everything to take care of the life God has given us. It is caring for oneself. Care for your body, your health, and your spiritual and mental well-being. It makes us watch what we eat and drink because we care about ourselves. Jesus encourages us to love ourselves. "Love your neighbor as yourself". If you can't love yourself, you can't love anybody. Love for self is what teaches us not to do to others what we won't want others to do to us. It also teaches us that if it is good for us, it will be good for others.

Self-worship, on the other hand, borders on self-worship. It is the mother of selfishness. Selfishness is characterized by a concern for one's welfare and a disregard for the welfare of others. Selfishness does not care about other people's feelings. As long as he is okay, others can go to hell. Such people are horrible people to love. They will take from you and never give you anything in return. Mr. Selfish will break your heart. Watch how he treats people. Does he show genuine concern for the feelings of others? Is he kind? Is he considerate? Do people speak well of him in this regard? Or does he worship himself so much that you are not in the picture of his plans? Think about this seriously. Mr. Selfish is stingy and self-centered. He cannot love another. When they become husbands, they won't change. They will take everything and leave peanuts for the wife and children. Watch them: they are robust, healthy, and cared for while their wives and children are haggard, unkempt, and hungry. Their idea of being the head of the family is to have the largest share of everything and to give the remnants to their family. Family Headship is about laying yourself down for the life, happiness, and comfort of others. It's about sacrifice. Mr. Selfish hates the word "sacrifice" unless he is on the receiving end of it. He is not the man you are looking for.

MR CONTROL FREAK

8. Mr. Control Freak

What does it mean to be a control freak? It means being overly possessive of others. A control freak wants to have you all to himself. He wants to own you. He wants your entire life to revolve around him. He wants to possess you so that you can't do anything without him. He is obsessively jealous and manipulative. Such men won't let you have friends. They are constantly monitoring your movements, keeping track of your affairs. They want to know who you are talking to on the phone and why you are so happy talking to them. They are always around you like bodyguards. They won't give you a chance to catch your breath. You can't travel without him. He is always imagining things. He is crazy! Crazy about you to a point it has become unhealthy and dangerous. Such individuals can resort to violence to win the affection of their target. A relationship is not about control; it's about freedom. Freedom to be our authentic selves before another. A control freak needs help, and you are not going to be able to give him that help. He needs to see a Psychiatrist. A doctor. They are love addicts. Never having enough love. Always asking for more love, more attention, more loyalty, more, more, more!. Yes, a man can be in love and exhibit that affection at times, but not excessively. Not to the extent he wants to turn you into his personal property. You can't go out, you can't come in, you can't talk, you can't keep quiet, and you can't do anything until they say so. If he behaves like this when you are not yet married, he will likely be even worse after marriage. Then you won't be able to leave the house without signing an agreement paper, nor can you have friends. This is not love. This is bondage! Be free from Mr. Control Freak today!

9. Mr. Vagabond

What does it mean to be a vagabond? It means to move about aimlessly or without any destination, often in search of food or employment. A vagabond is a wanderer who has no established residence or visible means of support. He is a drifter. A tramp. He does not belong anywhere. He is rootless. He has no sense of affiliation with anything authentic. He has no spiritual authority or any form of authority over his life. To him, anything goes. Before committing to a relationship, take the time to get to know who he is. A person is defined not just by what they call themselves, but also by where they come from and what they are connected to. His family. His roots. Let us narrow this issue down to the subject at hand.

Mr. Vagabond belongs to nothing. He is a rebel. He is subject to no man nor God. He has neither a Pastor nor a spiritual adviser. He does what he likes. He has no rule guiding what he does. To him, if he wants to do a particular thing, good or bad, then it is right to do it. He is warped in his thinking. How can you control such a person or call him back to order when he derails? Who will you report him to for caution and to prevent his excesses, since he is subject to no one? How can he obey the word of God to love and be faithful to his wife when he does not believe in God, nor is he subject to His authority? He is a loose cannon; take cover! If he is not committed to God or a church or religious body, how can he commit to you?

A vagabond has no authority because he is subject to no authority. To have authority is to be under authority. Ask him "who is your father? Who inspires you?" Who speaks into your life? Who is your Pastor (or Minister)?" "What do you believe in?" If he can't answer these questions correctly, then he is not your man. Avoid him. And it becomes worse when a vagabond becomes rich. Then he is proud and uncontrollable. He will wreck your life. Don't let his money deceive you. Flee from such.

10. **Mr. Unforgiving**

Unforgiveness is a manifestation of man's fallen nature. Sometimes it is difficult to forgive a wrong that has been done to us. It is difficult but not impossible. If it were impossible to overlook offences, Jesus would not have commanded us to forgive others their sins against us. He even said that if we don't forgive others their sins against us, God the Father will not forgive us our wrongdoing. Yes, it is hard sometimes to let the feeling go and move on with life. But it remains the only option. An unforgiving man is an impossible person to relate to. We are all human and are bound to make mistakes. We need to be given another chance to make amends for the wrongs we have done to others. Forgiveness is how we get another opportunity to right our wrongs. An unforgiving man cannot be in a relationship for too long. He finds it difficult to move past a past offense and let go of the pain. His heart is bitter, and that bitterness shows up in his expressions. At the slightest provocation, he exhumes the corpses of past wrongs and makes them alive again.

Such people, when they are non–verbal, are hazardous. They can kill. Don't marry a man who cannot forgive. He will continue to see you with the eyes of anger, bitterness, and soon hatred. He is vindictive and specializes in vendetta. Any man who won't let you make your mistakes and learn from them, who is not patient, tolerant, and magnanimous in heart, is not the man to catch. To be in such a relationship is to risk a lifetime of unhappiness and abuse. If he can't forgive you, no matter what you did, he can't marry you. And even when he does, it will be a lifetime of punishment and misery.

This, however, is not a license to offend others. There are offences that, even when they are forgiven, the relationship cannot continue. E.g. Infidelity. Don't expect a man to stay in a relationship with a partner who has been repeatedly unfaithful to him. He is not under any obligation to continue in that relationship. He has the right to end it if he can't live with it. But I know men who, despite that, can still forgive because the partner has genuinely changed. However you see it, no true love can last without forgiveness.

11 Mr. Irresponsible

A responsible person knows and fulfills their duties and responsibilities. For example, it is a man's duty to provide for his family. That is what it takes to be called a MAN. He is not fit to be in a relationship, let alone a marriage, when he does not have a visible, predictable means of income. If he can't pay his bills, he can't handle a woman. Avoid the wrong man. Next thing you know, the two of you are now depending on your next pay packet. You go to a restaurant to eat, and he allows you to pay the bill. He is always borrowing money from you with promises of paying back (which he never does). Some even go to the extent of stealing from their partners when asking and borrowing doesn't work. Before you take a man seriously, he must have a plan, visible actions, and proof to show that he is not lazy and idle. That he is willing and able to take responsibility for his family. The bible warns that he who fails to provide for his family (that would be his wife and kids) is worse than an infidel and has denied the faith. 1st Timothy 5:8 One of the tenets of the Christian faith is responsibility for others.

Mr. Irresponsible is always full of words and no action. He is always boasting about other people's wealth, maybe family members. He believes in luxury without labor, pleasure without effort, comfort without commitment to duty. Once little money gets into his hands, he blows it on useless and egocentric wastes. He likes to look rich without being rich. He has no problem with borrowing to eat. He can borrow to impress and later get into trouble. Marrying him is marrying a liability. You will continue to carry him all your days. He won't work. He is choosy about work. He is proud and won't serve anybody. He won't listen to advice. He prefers to sit down and collect free money. He may be marrying you because of your money. He confuses you with words and ends up contributing nothing. He is not your man. Your man won't sit down and let you feed him. No! Not when he is still physically able and mentally sound. He will get out and work, bringing substance to make your life sweet and enjoyable.

Avoid MR MARRY ME

12.Mr. Marry Me

Who is Mr. Marry Me? He is driven by a desire to get married, not a desire for a relationship. He is interested in marriage for many other reasons that have nothing to do with love and romance. Such people marry because their peers are getting married. So he goes out to marry whoever it is that comes his way, just to prove a point. Another reason such people marry is to fulfill the wish of either their parents or someone influential in their lives. There is nothing wrong with that, but usually such marriages fail. Love must be the only primary reason for a valid marriage. You can survive with love and nothing else, but you can't survive with everything else without love. It can't work. Mr. Marry Me wants to get married. Perhaps to obtain a visa so that he can travel abroad. So, they rush any person they see to the Priest or Pastor for a blessing and to receive the marriage certificate. They need that certificate to qualify for a VISA. Others may marry to have children. To them, a wife is just a child-making machine, and when she fails to produce, the marriage is terminated. It has nothing to do with love. Some also marry to inherit certain property. If they don't marry, they can't inherit what someone (maybe a parent) left for them.

Typically, marriages that fall into the above categories tend to experience difficulties and often fail. Love remains the most essential foundation for a lasting marriage. Some also say "Marry Me" because of what you have, which they stand to gain from marrying you. Perhaps a family wealth, possession, or connection to someone in the family. People marry for many reasons. Some men marry ladies for political reasons. It's not about love. Soon, both parties are married but hate each other.

Others say "Marry Me" as a trap to get a woman in bed with him, only to break the engagement once he has gotten what he wants. Look for a man who wants to marry because he loves you and wants to spend the rest of his life with you. Such men abound if you know where to look.

In the next section, we will discuss where to find good men

A fisherman knows where and when to find the right type of fish. But first, let us complete our discussion about men you don't want to catch.

13. Mr. User

He is not interested in you; he is interested in what he can use you to achieve for himself. You are just a tool in his hand to achieve his mission. Once your usefulness expires, he dumps you. He may not even be physically attracted to you as such. He is just pretending. He has seen other uses for you, sometimes economic uses. Once he achieves his goal with your help, he will drop you. He is Mr user. He steals your ideas and visions, as well as your contacts. He sees you as a stepping stone to his ambitions. The key is to pay him back with his own coin, use him to get what you want, and dump him fast.

14 Mr. Promise and Fail.

He has no value for words. Integrity is not one of his strong points. Don't expect him to keep his promise to you; they are all lies. He is a liar; he lives a lie, and he is a lie. He makes promises he knows he can never fulfill. When he tells you to marry him, he does not mean it. It is just one of those things he says. Everywhere he goes, he leaves a trail of heartbreak and hurt. This is not a person to take seriously in ordinary life issues, let alone marriage. How can you marry a man who has no respect for his words? He even frowns in amazement when you make too much fuss about his unkept promises; to him, words mean nothing. How can you fall in love with that kind of man? All he will cause you is untold pain and bitterness. A good man never promises what he cannot do, and even when he does make a promise to you, he will strive to keep it.

15 Mr. Taken.

Not all men are available for catching. In this game of men hunting, you need to know who to take and who to leave. Mr. Taken belongs to another woman. He can never be yours. This book is not about helping you snatch another woman's man; it is about showing you how to catch your own. Who is Mr. Taken? He is Mr. Married and happy. Mr. Engaged and unavailable. Don't play the game of man snatching, no woman has ever played that game and did not have her hands burned. It's a lost war, don't fight it. Even if you succeed and do snatch him from her, be sure that the seed you sow to others, you will surely live to reap.

First of all, you will never really have him. Just like you snatched him from another, someone else will snatch him from you. What goes around comes around. Don't be tempted. You are worth more than that. Don't wish he were yours; it's a dangerous way to live. Forget him; wish them both the best and move on to what God has for you. Sometimes Mr. Taken tries to become Mr. One Night Stand. He is taken, but he still wants to play around. He is happily married but he still wants to convince you that it is you he wants. He is tired of his marriage. It is all lies. If he really wanted you, he would end the marriage and come for you. But he won't. All he wants is to make you his whore. His secret sex escapade. His mistress. Refuse to be a second fiddle when God designed you to be someone's number one. Why consent to be an illegitimate lover to a man you will never have and risk the shame and regret that it brings, when God has kept someone ten thousand times better for you? You are worth more than that. Don't let any man use you only to dump you when the going gets rough. Believe God for your own. God has a man for you. Don't fall into the trap of Mr. Taken. All he wants is to play with you. How can love be so sweet and yet so wrong? If it is true love, why should it be hidden? There is no shame in love, but if it is shameful, it can't be true love. It's not worth it, my beloved. God has something much better for you.

SAY NO TO MR WRONG AND SAY YES TO MR RIGHT

Chapter Four

THE TYPE OF MAN TO CATCH

Good men are not scarce. All you need to do is find them. But to find them, you need to know where to look. Every fisherman knows that to catch fish, you need to go where the fish are. It makes sense—a lot. Don't say that because you can't find good fish on this side of the lake, there are no fish in the lake. You are simply fishing in the wrong spot. If it's not working where you are fishing, change location. For example, no matter how skillful you are in the art of fishing, you can't catch a shark in a pool! To catch a shark, you must go where sharks swim. The type of fish you want to catch determines where you are to fish.

Another point to consider is not only the place but also the time. You must be at the right place at the right time. To be successful in fishing, you must know.

(i) The type of fish you want to catch

(ii). Where to go and find them

(iii). When to go there

(iv.) What type of bait do you need to have? Not all bait will catch all kinds of fish. There is no one–size–fits–all strategy for all kinds of fish.

So, to start, let's find out what type of man you should be looking to catch.

What kind of man should you look for?

I. **He must have a relationship with God.** Why is this important? You need a man who knows God and walks with Him. You need a man who will help you find your destiny in God. The sole purpose of having a man in your life is to have a spiritual connection to God. He must have a testimony. An encounter. He must be saved. If he is not, then pray that he is. This is so important. Who you submit yourself to as your head needs to be subject to Christ. Here is my rule: Don't follow a man who does not follow Christ. 1 Corinthians 11:1. He must be a lover and imitator of God. One who inspires you to get closer to God and become a better person.

II **He must have a Vision** – A man without a vision is as dangerous as a car speeding down the road without a driver. Vision gives direction to life. Vision is a sense of where you are going. Knowing where you are going and how to get there. Before you can say "yes" to his charms, ask him, "What is your vision?" Where do you hope to be five to ten to twenty years from now? How do you intend to get there?" Vision is not just seeing where you are going but knowing how you will get there. The word of God makes it clear that **"where there is no vision the people perish" Proverbs 29:18.** To "perish" here means to cast off restraint; To be without direction and control; To wander to any direction; A man needs to have a sense of direction.. He must have a vision. A dream. A life goal. An understanding of his life assignment. If you are coming to help him achieve something, he must at least know what he is trying to achieve.

III **He must know his Purpose.** What is purpose? Purpose means intention, Aim, and Reason for being. Everything created was created for a purpose—a reason. God is a God of purpose and design. He does everything with a purpose in mind. He is the Maker of all men. For every man and woman created by God, there is a divine purpose. Every man should seek God to discover His purpose for him. You see, knowing your purpose is how you learn to understand why you are the way you are. Once a person discovers their divine purpose from God, they begin to live a purpose-driven life. A life that is bound to become a successful life. A man of purpose exudes confidence. He knows who he is, and he knows what it takes to get where he wants to go. He is not beating about the bush. He is constant and focused. Knowing him is an adventure. This is one reason he needs to know God, because only God, the creator of man, knows man and can reveal His purpose for that person. If he does not know his purpose, he won't know where you fit in his life.

IV. **He must Have Integrity:** What is Integrity? It means unity; Agreement; Wholeness; An undivided or unbroken completeness; or totality with nothing wanting. It also means moral soundness; unchanging in character, content, and physical makeup. A man of integrity means what he says and says what he means. His actions align with his words; they are consistent. He does not say one thing and mean something else. He does not lie with his mouth. A lie is simply a conscious concealing of a truth or fact. A man of integrity is constant. He is reliable. He is trustworthy. He is the same everywhere he goes. He is not wearing a mask. He is real. He strives to give his best effort in everything he does. He does not make promises he cannot keep. Even when he does make one, he will strive to keep it. He will never break your heart. If he is not into you (or interested in you), he won't give you the impression that he is. No innuendoes and subliminal messages. His "yes" is his "yes", his "no" is his "no". Such men are easy to find if you look in the right place. He is always pursuing a new task. He is busy. His mind is constantly creating new ways of getting things done. He loves to work and gives his best to everything he does, including his relationships with those he loves. If he tells you he loves you, he does. No pretense, no falsehood. Look for such men.

THE TYPE OF MAN TO CATCH continued

V. **He must be diligent and hardworking:** Man was made to work. That's what gives him a sense of worth. No normal man will enjoy sitting idle and doing nothing. Have you seen a man who loves work and gives himself to a task till it's done with much enthusiasm? That's your man! You don't want anything to do with a lazy idler who seeks nothing but undue pleasures and gratifications. After God created the first man, the first thing He gave him was work to do. Genesis 2:15 "And the Lord God took the man and put him into the Garden of Eden to dress it and to keep it." He was a garden dresser and a watchman. He had work to do. God did not give him a wife until He gave him a work. It was while he was busy working that God observed, "It is not good that the man should be alone. I will make him a help meet for him" Genesis 2:18, the word "help" suggests something. It means he has work to do, which he can't do alone, so "I will give him someone who will help him do it". Simple. An idle man does not need wife. He needs a job. Idleness and laziness lead to poverty and lack. You don't want a man who will plunge you and your children into poverty.

VI. **He must appeal to you sexually:** What does it mean to have sexual appeal? It means to have sexual attraction. It talks about being sexually attracted to someone of the opposite sex. It also talks about charm, attractiveness that stimulates. He must be able to turn you on. This is so important. Many women are miserable in their marriages because they find themselves tied to someone they have no sexual attraction to. Sex appeal basically means desirability. Being desirable. Attractiveness to the opposite sex. There must be something about his personality that lights your fire. You see, one great ingredient for a lasting marriage is great sex. Great sex has everything to do with sexual appeal. If he does not turn you on, stimulate you sexually by his looks, his voice, his physique, his manner of life, his eyes, his masculinity, his character, etc. If nothing about him stirs you to want him, he can't be your man. You will be married and yet not fulfilled. It is neglecting this point that has led to many cases of marital unfaithfulness on the part of some women.

Now I am not advocating negative vices such as lust, lasciviousness, concupiscence, and immorality. I am not suggesting that women go about drooling each time they see attractive men, far from it. I am basically saying that to be happy with your catch, he must be totally what you want, in fact, everything you want in a man. You must be totally satisfied with him. The frustration in this is that most times, men who possess sexual appeal are either not available (because some fast sister has grabbed him) or even when they are available, they are playboys. It's hard to find a smashing, dashing, ravishing young man who is not tied up somewhere these days. This is why most ladies prefer to settle for anything they can get. But I still believe that if we are patient and trust in God, He will give us the desire of our hearts. Trust Him. Don't be in haste. That man of your dreams can be yours — if you know where to look.

VII He needs to have a good sense of humor: What does it mean to have a good sense of humor? It is the trait of appreciating and being able to express the humorous. It means being able to see the funny side of life. Not one to take life too seriously. One who can laugh at a joke. One who knows how to take away tension. A man who can laugh and make people laugh is an interesting person to be around. You don't have to be able to make people laugh to have a sense of humor. But you must be able to see the funny in everything and laugh. Laughter works like medicine to the soul. *Proverbs 17:22. "A merry heart doeth good like medicine".* Medicine is good for your body; laughter is good for your soul. People who claim to always look serious are hardly that serious. I realized that one trait you will notice in great people up close is their unbelievable sense of humor. You want to be happy in your marriage. You want to have moments of laughter and joy. You need a man who can laugh and make you feel at ease in his presence. Not a tyrant or a dictator. A friend.

VIII **He needs to be serious-minded:** Too much of everything can be bad. Yes he needs to have a good sense of humor but he also needs not to overdo it. A serious-minded person is able to make the right decisions when he/she need to. Serious-mindedness talks about soberness. Knowing when to stop. It talks about thoughtfulness – acting with or showing thought and good sense. Being sensible. Making the right decisions. Pursuing things that are important. Being serious-minded means having a good sense of priority. Not dwelling on trivia or fantasies. Yes, he needs to have a sense of humor but he also needs to know when to do the right things. For example, he needs to be able to take you seriously. He is mature enough to know what to joke with and what not to joke with. He is balanced.

IX. **He must agree with you on key points:** You must be compatible. Compatibility is so important in choosing a life partner. To be compatible basically means to be well matched; to be agreeable with; to be of like mind; to have something in common with another; to be able to function together without needing to adjust or be modified; to be well matched, existing together harmoniously. It also means to have similar dispositions and tastes. The bible makes this clear by saying, "Can two walk together if they do not agree?" Amos 3:3.

BASIC AREAS OF AGREEMENT

Most relationships fail because of a lack of compatibility. They try to force a square peg into a round hole. It can't work. The square peg will be destroyed, and the round hole will be damaged. Relationships work when both parties sing from the same book and on the same key. Harmony is the right word. Do you know your type of person? This is crucial. Basic Areas of Agreement:

a. Beliefs: He must be of the same faith as you. It does not work for a Christian to seek a relationship with a man who does not believe in Christ. There is no agreement, and so it will fail. You must believe the same thing.

b. Vision: Two of you must agree on the vision. His vision must not conflict with yours. You see, marriage is actually a union of vision, ideas, and beliefs. Do you have a vision for your life? Do you know your man's vision for life? Are you both pursuing the same thing?

c. Style: You must both strike the same tone on style. Manner of operations. How do you do things? If you are the creative type, look for someone with a flair for art and expression. Even if he is not the artistic type, he should at least be able to appreciate the things you find fascinating.

d. Background: Where you come from is also important. Your history, experiences. Where you have been, it's so sweet to meet someone who seems to have almost the same experience and background as you. It makes communication so sweet, you don't have to explain everything.

e. Class: He must come from your class. Your rank in life. Marry your class. Does he speak your language? Is he exposed to the things you are exposed to? Do you belong to the same social class? For example, a graduate should marry a graduate or a soon-to-be graduate. Water must always find its level.

f. Physical compatibility: He must have an agreeable genotype, one that agrees with your status. If, for example, you are "AA" and he his "AA" or "AS" or even "SS", you will not have sicklers as children. But if you are "AS" and he is "AS", your chances of having "SS" sickle cell children are there. I am not really an expert in this, so confirm your status first. Do you know your genotype status?

X. **He must have a good report** among people who know him: Reputation is what people say about you. What you are known for. Jesus asked His disciples this question: "Whom do men say that I am, the Son of man?" Matt 16:13. Why did He ask this question? Because it matters what people say about you. They are not always right, but most of the time they are. Reputation means notoriety. What is one notorious for? A man with a reputation for promiscuity is not who you are looking for. He will ruin your life. Reputation is the general estimation that the public has of a person. Public report of a person. In choosing leaders over God's flock, it is recommended that he must be blameless, "moreover, he must have a good report of them which are without, lest he fall into reproach and the snare of the devil." 1 Timothy 3:2, 7. What are people saying about him? Everybody cannot be wrong or right. Sadly, I have found that people are hardly wrong. If they say someone is bad, study closely and you will find why they said so. Granted, it is possible that people change. It is possible that what people are still saying about him is from his past life. But if he honestly decides to make a change for the better and show through acts of consistent honesty and goodness that he has changed, soon people will change their minds. Does what people say matter? It may not always be true, but there is no smoke without fire. Beyond reputation is character. Reputation is who people say you are; they can be wrong, but character is who you are when no one is watching. It shows up in a repeated pattern of behavior. It is consistent. The danger here is that some people are so good at guarding their reputation and maintaining a good report in public, while their character, which they really are, is horrible. So listen to the people and do your own investigation. Don't take anything on face value.

XI **He must be physically sound:** He must be physically able to be in a relationship. He must not have a terminal disease that will soon or surely take his life. This is really difficult to say. Love is such a beautiful thing. It does not care about the other person's physical disqualification. It is drawn to that inner person who lives in the body. This is why normal people fall in love with many people who are physically challenged. Love is a miracle. But generally, you must know the health status of the man you are dating. Knowing the truth gives you options. You should know his genotype and his blood group. His HIV status – this is so important. If he is HIV positive and you are not, at least you should know so that you can decide whether you want to go on with him, in spite of that, because you love him. At least you should know. It's not fair to know one's HIV status to be positive and hide it from a loved one, all in the bid not to lose him or her. You must also know how healthy he is. Does he have any infections, or is he struggling with a hereditary disease like diabetes? If he is seriously sick, you may need to take stock of what you are dealing with. If you can stick with him, great, but if you can't, don't feel guilty about it. You need a healthy man to build a healthy family. This is so important. You must know the physical condition of the man you are trying to keep. Bring up these issues in your next meeting. Do it lovingly and wisely. Don't force it, but be firm about it. It could be an issue of life or death.

XII. **He must be Kind and Generous:** A kind and generous man is a lover of people. He is hospitable, compassionate, and always seeking ways to help people. Such a man will do you well all the days of your life. Look for a man who loves to give. He is not stingy and selfish. Does he buy you gifts? Does he seek means to lavish you with things? Even when he can't afford it, does he go through pains just to make you happy? Is he a giver? Is he kind to people? Is he the type who will not hold back any good thing from the object of his affection? How a man treats you before marrying you is how he will treat you after marrying you. If he is stingy and full of excuses, that won't change after the marriage, it may grow worse. On the other hand, if he is generous and kind, that won't change in marriage. True love is a giver. If a man is truly in love with a woman, he opens up his hand to her, holding nothing back. That is the power of love. You need a man who will do everything in his power to make you happy. You can give and not love, but you cannot love and not give. Having seen some of the things to look for in your man, we will proceed to talk about WHERE TO FIND GOOD MEN.

85

86

WHERE CAN A WOMAN FIND A GOOD MAN?

Chapter Five

WHERE TO FIND GOOD MEN.

Like I said earlier, good men are not scarce; you just need to know where to look for them. I guarantee you, they are there. Where do you find good men? After careful study on this area, I discovered two points: Where and When.

"Where" talks about place while "when" talks about timing. This is an important law of fishing. You must go where the fish are and you must go when they are there. To catch your man, you must go to where good men are.

i. **In the Church:** Your chances of finding a good man in the congregation of God's people are very high. The more they are in number, the greater the chances of finding good men there. A good man has a relationship with God and goes to church regularly to worship and serve Him. This is his custom. Every good man has a custom, a habit, a fashion, something regular with someone. For example, on Sunday morning, you know exactly where to find a good man, in Church. Not playing football with friends, nor slouching in front of the TV set watching movies. He will be at church worshipping and praising God. He will be a member of his church. A worker in the church, committed to the growth and expansion of God's kingdom. He will be there to attend all the services. So go to church. Not to catch a man but to find the God that holds him. If you please God, He will give you His best man. Go to church, that is where good men gather. Join a department or service arm. Get committed there, and soon something will happen.

Caution: If you are not of God, if you do not have a true testimony of salvation, you don't know Jesus as your Lord and Savior, you have no business going to the church to seek out a godly man. Godly men are reserved for godly women. So go to church and seek God, and he will change your life and later give you the man of your desire. "Delight yourself also in the Lord your God and He shall give thee the desires of thine heart" Psalm 37:4 . Don't seek the man, seek God and He will put you in the heart of the man. It's good to add another note of caution, not all the men you see in church are good men. There are wolves in sheep's clothing, looking for whom to devour. Be careful about who you open up to. Watch their fruit, their lifestyle outside the church. Be wise, not all that glitters is gold.

ii. **In the Workplace:** No real man will find it comfortable to sit idly at home when he has work to do. After God, what a man worships most is his work. That is what gives him a sense of self-worth and esteem. He is his work. If he is not at home, he is out there, in his workplace, trying to make a living and by so doing, make a difference. Good men are at work. In the banks, in the media houses, in the hospitals, in the marketplaces, on the bus, on the motorbike (okada), in the field. You will find good men striving to make an impact on something worthwhile. Where are all the good men? Well, from morning to evening, from Monday to Friday (and some Saturdays), every good man can be found somewhere, working or learning to work. The type of fish you want to catch defines where you go to fish. Big fish don't swim in a small pool. Ruth operated this law and got hooked in no time. She went to the field where men worked, and while she labored, she was noticed and soon Boaz, the owner of the field, saw her and fell for her. Ruth2:1-23. Don't sit all day at home, watching movies and doing nothing, and expect to catch your man. Get out there, where men are, and be discovered. Most women were hooked at their place of work. While distinguishing themselves in their work, others saw them. Nothing trips a man like a woman who is not afraid to work. It means she will not be a burden but an added resource.

iii. **In the School or Any Learning Environment:** Good men know the value of education. They know the importance of personal development. They know the value of education. You will find them in schools, trying to advance their lives. So, go to school. Get a degree, two or more. Read widely. Work yourself out as you strive to enlarge your base. Many people have been hooked while pursuing an academic dream. Some men even come to these campuses to fish out good wife material. School is good in that it creates more playing space for you to maneuver. You meet so many prospects, and soon enough, after graduation, wedding bells begin to ring. Go where your life is going. School creates that needed momentum you need to launch you into the marketplace of possibilities.

iv. **In the Military and armed forces:** Good men can also be found in the army, in the forces. The tendency of the army marrying the army is very great. Men like to marry their own. Do you want to marry someone from the military? Then join the military in whatever capacity that suits you.

v. **In Social gatherings:** You are bound to meet good men in some good social functions. Weddings, birthday parties, child naming ceremonies, marriage wine carrying, etc. The snag here is that you also find the wrong men here. So be on your guard. Be watchful and vigilant. Above all, don't lose control of yourself. Don't overdo anything. Be temperate and calculative; eyes are watching you. Dress impressively. Don't dress to kill. Dress to save life. Dress the way you want to be addressed. Be regal and together. Your type will find you. In choosing social functions to attend, know who is throwing the bash. Is he or she a person of good reputation? A party of thieves will attract thieves. You can't find good men there. Good men go to where good men gather. Birds of the same feather flock together. That you were invited shouldn't be a guarantee that you must be there. Be selective. Go where you will be proud to be seen. Many have been beautifully hooked during such social events. So keep your ears to the ground. Be on the lookout. Don't go to everybody's party. To get the type of people you are seeking, go to their parties. Go prepared to be seen by the right eye, the right man. Attend the parties of the kind of people you are seeking

vi. **In Leadership Places –** Solving Problems: You will find good men giving leadership. They know how to influence people in the direction of a task. He is a problem–solver. He is a leader. Anywhere you see leadership and followership, you will see good men. They are good followers and make good leaders. Join a movement. Something geared towards rendering service to mankind. A cause. A society development group. N.G.O. Good men are always seeking to join something where they can make a difference. Civil societies, networks, welfare organizations, etc. Find a good cause and support, and soon good men will see you.

vii. **Under an Authority:** Every good man knows the value of being under authority. They are not rebellious and self-willed. They submit to something higher. He has a boss, a leader, a senior officer. Any man who won't stay under authority can never be in authority. Look for a man who honors and reveres constituted authority. Don't submit to a man who will not submit to authority

There are other places you can find good men. Going to a place like a nightclub is not a very sure place to find good men. They don't do night parties, and even if they do, it is clean and decent. The chances of finding him in a pub (beer parlor) are also very slim, although miracles can happen! What about on a plane or bus trip? Can a good man be found there? Yes and no. It is a risk but like I said, miracles can happen. If you look well, you can find good men almost anywhere.

Viii **Online, Social Media:** in chat groups, reputable dating sites, or just on Facebook or other social networks. Many have been hitched with their dream person from such places, even though the chances of connecting with the wrong people online are very high. Tread with extreme caution, don't take unnecessary risks with your life. Observe the following rules for safe online affairs;

Do not expose yourself too much online; the less information available about you, the better. Just upload some very nice pictures of yourself on your profile page with limited information about yourself. Be findable!

If you connect with someone online, don't believe anything people display about themselves online. People lie, especially on the internet. So take everything with a pinch of salt. Until you they prove themselves.

Never ever travel to another state to meet a so-called lover you met online. Let him be the one to travel to meet you.

If you must meet, meet in an open public place where you feel safe.

Apply all necessary precautions to protect yourself. Do a lot of research on people. The more you know, the safer you are.

Beware of online love scammers who use fake pictures and profiles to scam unsuspecting victims. Always insist on face-to-face video calls to establish that the person in the profile picture is indeed the person chatting with you. The fake ones will put up excuses why their phone camera is faulty and won't work, and so forth.

Never reveal your location or where you live to strangers.

If you must go and visit this new friend, go with someone.

All these are necessary precautions to follow at first until a level of trust has been established.

If you are prayerful, awake, and sensitive, you can find him just about anywhere. The key is to make yourself findable by being in the right place at the right time. In the next section, we will discuss what you need to be to catch your man. Qualities you must possess to be successful in this area.

BECOMING THE WOMAN HE IS SEARCHING FOR

Chapter Six

WHAT YOU NEED TO BE TO CATCH THE RIGHT MAN

One central principle of fishing and hunting is that to catch prey, you must be highly adaptive and able to know what is required of you.

What is it in a woman that takes any man captive?

To catch a man, there are things you must be:

1 YOU MUST BE BEAUTIFUL

Yes, you must be beautiful. Man is a visual being. In other words, he is motivated by what he sees. A man may forgive a woman for falling short in other qualities as long as she is beautiful. So, what is beauty? Personal appearance. Beauty is often associated with being very attractive or seductive. Appealing to the eyes and other senses. Beauty is also defined as the qualities that give pleasure to the senses. Beauty must be raw, uncut, stark, and powerfully impressive. Women are created to be beautiful. Looking at the body configuration of a woman, you can tell that the Designer deliberately molded her to be a creature to be desired. You are beautiful. You have qualities that delight the senses, which can excite intellectual or emotional admiration. You are supposed to be admired and desired. Beauty, they say, is in the eye of the beholder. Part of God's plan to enhance the aesthetic qualities of life is creating woman. Without women, life would be colorless, meaningless, and boring. Accept your place in God's creative plan. Beauty should not be viewed as a negative thing or a vice, belonging only to the depraved, mundane and ungodly.

Beauty is of God. Rachel was beautiful and well favored. Beauty commands natural favor. Genesis 29:17. Consequently Jacob loved her and served her father. He labored for her for seven years, and to him, it seemed like a few days. That is the power of beauty. It sends the man to work. To catch a man's heart and keep him for life, you must make maintaining your beauty a life goal. One excellent quality Esther possessed that gave her the seat of Queen was her beauty. "And the maid was fair and beautiful" Esther 2:7. Once the king saw her, he could not resist her beauty. "And the king loved Esther above all women and she obtained grace and favor in his sight more than all the virgins; so that he set the royal crown upon her head and made her queen instead of Vashti". Esther 2:17

Beauty is power. It can take the strongest men captive and loosen the loins of kings. Beauty commands favor. It throws a charm on the man, as an enthralled admirer. He is subject to you to do all your whims and caprices. Just have mercy. In the Song of Solomon, we read more about this point. This verse reflects the kind of impact beauty can have on a man: *Thou art beautiful, O my love, as Tirzah, comely as Jerusalem, terrible as an army with barriers. Turn away thine flashing eyes from me, for they have overcome me. Thy hair is as a flock of goats that appear from Gilead. Songs of Solomon 6:4,5*

"Turn away your flashing eyes from me, for they have overcome me." This is powerful. Beauty casts a spell on the beholder. It has an overcoming effect. Women need to know the impact their beauty already has on men; they won't need to bend over to please them. You are already in charge; he is waiting for your next instruction. As a rule, don't pursue an affair with a man who is not enchanted by your beauty. You won't have much power over him. He must be enthralled, captivated, and suspended in your beauty. That is your true power. Now let's make this clear. There is a difference between being beautiful and being enchanting. It is he who finds you the most attractive person he has ever seen, who your beauty can enchant. I have found that there are two types of beauty: General beauty and Exclusive beauty

a. General beauty is that which appeals to all. When a woman is said to be "drop-dead gorgeous," you don't need to be a beauty expert to acknowledge such beauty. This beauty is objective, obvious to see.

b. Exclusive beauty is that which is hidden. Only to be discovered by those who search. It is the beauty that is relative. It does not appeal to all but it does appeal to some. This kind of beauty is not readily apparent. One eye discovers it, and soon others acknowledge her. This beauty is subjective. Whatever category you belong to, you are beautiful in the eyes of someone. Every woman was designed to meet a man's need somewhere. So if one does not acknowledge your beauty, you were not made for him. Do not let anyone feel like you are not what they want, but they are compelled to cope with their decision to be with you. Never put yourself in that situation.

2 You must be Regal – You are a queen, someone's queen. Carry yourself as such. Dress for the person you're looking for. To be regal means to be imperial. To be majestic. To be royal. It means to have a sense of royalty and carriage. To be treated like a queen, you must learn to act like one.

Dressing: One way to show yourself regal is in your dressing. You are what you wear. Don't put on things that cheapen you in the eyes of men. Dress in such a way that says "I know who I am and

I want to be treated with respect." People will treat you the way they see you treat yourself. Who you are is who you will attract. Always be in your best behavior. Think before you speak. Do everything in your power not to be dragged into a senseless dispute. Don't let your name be mentioned for evil or anything vulgar and foolish. Be choosy about the company you keep. Appear regal and self-confident by so doing, you make yourself seem destined for the crown. People will naturally assume the role of subjects around you in response to your charm. Areas to work on:

a. Your manner of speech: Talk like a queen. Never speak defeat and failure. Speak faith. Choose words that best represent your feelings. Words that you would like to be quoted.

b. Behavior: Be kind and generous. Always ready to stoop down and give a helping hand to those in need. Never speak words that slander, but speak words that build up. Act the part, twenty four/ seven. Be self-aware. Don't look desperate and greedy. Put it away. Be content with who you are and what you have. Behave like a queen, above gossip, above criticism, above scandal. Strive to be perfect.

C Dressing: Dress honorably. Exude absolute attraction without making it so obvious. Always seem unaware of the impact your outfit is having on people. Avoid loose and trampy dressing.

D Carriage – This means the characteristic way one bears their body, Good Posture. Walk smart. Don't drag your feet. Don't scatter your steps. Walk knowing you are important. You are a queen, someone's queen. Push your chest out and walk with an air of self-possession and purpose. Always appear to perform for an invisible audience. Carry yourself with dignity and soon everyone including your man will treat you the same. To catch your man, you must make yourself seem more than just any woman to him. Put him in a position where he will want to possess you for himself by the way you package yourself.

3 YOU MUST BE UNUSUAL

You must invest in Spectacle: The world hates the usual and mundane. A man gets bored easily when things appear usual and predictable. Don't just be any other girl, be the girl of his fantasies. Invest in spectacle. Spectacle makes you seem larger than life. Spectacle means an elaborate and remarkable display on a lavish scale. It is something or someone seen (especially a notable or unusual sight). Do everything not to appear usual and ordinary. Be creative in everything you do. Be different without being weird. Men like to be impressed. Practice the art of communication. Define yourself by the way you use words. Be better than anyone he has ever met. Dazzle him with symbols of power and wealth. Surround yourself with people of substance.

Be seen only with the best crowd. Just be different. Avoid the usual. Choose the right kind of colors that complement your skin color. Avoid drab and dull looks. You must master the use of colors. For example, use colors that draw attention to yourself. The eye predominates. People will respond more to the color than to the content. The visual contains great emotional power. Don't be swallowed up in the crowd; overwhelm it by appearing outstanding. Make every effort to ensure you never seem ordinary. Put in that extra effort that gets you noticed anywhere you go. Know what works for you and stick with it. Strive never to exude a wrong odor. Use perfumes and deodorants if you have to. Take good care of your skin and nails. Keep your hair tidy and neat. Wear things that enhance and complement your skin color.

Consult beauty experts if you have to. To catch a man, you must make him want to catch you.

4. You must be above average in intelligence: Beauty on its own is a great ally when catching men is the objective. But it has its limits. It only appeals to the sensual part of the man and his emotional part, too. But it does not deal with his intellectual needs. Combine beauty with intelligence, and you will take a nation captive. What is intelligence? It is the ability to process and manage information. To be of a quick mind. Astute: to be well informed.

To catch your man you can't afford to operate on average intelligence. The battles of life are fought and won in the mind. To be of weak, inferior mind is a liability in this business. Develop your rate of collecting, assimilating and acting upon information. You must demonstrate your wisdom by the way you speak and the choices you make. A man needs a woman who not only engages him emotionally but also intellectually. One who makes him think. One he can share his problems with and receive answers that work. Yes, men also have issues. Surprised? They don't know everything. They need answers to a lot of questions. You can be his adviser and confidant. Soon he learns to take his matters to you and by so doing, learns to depend on you. The key is to make a man rely on you. To increase your level of intelligence, you must!

a. Expose your mind to greater knowledge.

b. Always read a book. Never be without information. Develop and sustain an appetite for knowledge. Don't just clothe your body, clothe your mind too. Don't walk naked intellectually, not even beauty and charm can atone for that. Combine beauty with brains.

c. Expand your thinking level by stretching it with bigger and better ideas. Company with higher minds and be stretched.

d Attempt bigger tasks, newer and stronger than you. Problem solving stretches the mind. The more problems you solve the better your quality of thinking.

Make a note to be informed about everything. Any area of ignorance should be your next task for knowledge. The more you read, the better you think and the better you live. Be current with new trends. Be able to engage impressively in any kind of conversation without feeling a sense of inadequacy and lack of exposure Knowledge inspires confidence, and confidence exudes charm. It captivates.

5. You must master the art of seduction – Why? You ask, because if you don't know about seduction, you'll fall into the category of being a victim of seduction. Knowing about it protects you from being seduced and also helps you protect your man from other contenders. Seduction is a must. It is a reality we have come to accept, it is either you are seducing or you are being seduced. For us, mastering the art of seduction is about arming ourselves with the weapon that protects us from worldly seducers (you know their tricks and can escape their traps) and helps us keep our men. A godly woman must study how to keep her man continuously seduced by her charms. That is the only way she can protect him from outside intrusion. I have dedicated a section for this study in the ***"Laws of Seduction"***. Also, I deal more with this in the chapter ***"How to deal with the competition"***. However, for this study, the term seduction essentially means allurement, encompassing both attraction and temptation. It also implies enticement. The word "seduce" means to lead astray; to corrupt. It also means to induce someone to follow one's way. To influence by playing on one's emotions and weaknesses.

As a woman seeking to catch your man and keep him, you must know how and when to use this God-given power. There is a thin line between worldly seduction and godly seduction. While worldly seduction seeks to cause one to stray from the right path, godly seduction counteracts worldly influence and keeps one on track with God and His purpose. For example, while the devil uses female temptresses to seduce men out of God's holy ordinance of marriage, godly seduction nullifies that influence and keeps him on track with God. Knowing that whatever that strange woman seeks to offer him outside his marriage, his wife has it and more for him. You see, all the devil does is seek to offer us what we already have. It is dangerous to have something and not know you have it. If the man knows that in his woman is everything he will ever want in a woman, he will never be tempted to cheat. He does not need to. Find what they are offering him outside and give him something better than that and you can keep him. We must match seduction with seduction—more in the next section.

6. You must find your purpose and pursue it: You are a creature of purpose. You did not create yourself. God created you for a purpose. The word purpose means: aim, intention, goal, reason. Your first life quest is your quest for purpose. Know who you are and what you were made for. To find your purpose, you cannot ask another person you must ask God, your Maker.

Once you find the reason why you were made, you will know exactly what type of man to pray for. Purpose answers the question of which kind of man is meant for you. It also sets you on track on the path of destiny. Don't pursue men, pursue God and His plan for your life and soon men will be pursuing you to lay claim on you because you have become an asset. What is your life assignment? What is your ministry? What gifts and talents has God given you to invest? Are you occupied with it? Get busy now. A relationship is created to help fulfill your purpose, not the other way around. For every woman, God has made a man. Finding your purpose and walking in it exposes you to the eyes of your man. God knows how to arrange these things. Just trust him. Don't chase a man, chase your divine purpose, and your man will find you there.

7. You must be clean and decent: There is nothing a man hates like a lady who smells—one who has a foul odor. Be clean. This is so important. Don't look beautiful and smell like a pig! (Forgive my bluntness) Beauty will attract him, but foul odor and uncleanness may chase him away. The worst part is that he might not tell you. Beauty is not just about looking good outwardly; it is about feeling attractive because you know you have nothing to be afraid of. Please keep it clean! Here is some good advice from a man to you. Keep it clean. Clean is sexy and attractive. I don't need to go into details here, but if I must, I will say this much:

a.Wash your mouth regularly. Brush your teeth also. Avoid the tragedy of speaking and someone is trying to take cover! This goes to married women too. Keep your mouth clean. Brush your teeth before going to bed (because anything can happen). Be ready and vigilant. Brush it in the morning when you wake up, and try to rinse your mouth after each meal.

b. Wash your body regularly: don't allow sweat to gather on your body till it becomes stale and offensive. Have a beauty bath regularly.(Do I really need to say this?)

c. This goes to married women – keep all those private and essential areas clean. I mean your sexual organ and the environs. Please keep it clean and always fresh-smelling. Nothing destroys romance in the middle of the night like a foul, unwanted, crazy odor. Soon, the man begins to avoid sex because he doesn't have the courage to say to his beloved wife, "Go wash and come..." Since I am already down this road, I might as well go the whole hug. Use water to clean up and for a romantic effect, apply a sweet fragrance to your entire sexual apparatus. A good smell evokes sexual urges in a man. Good, clean smell. This is so important. I am risking my dignity as a man to tell you this. But I know you will understand. I am just trying to help. A good smell gives unbelievable confidence in every encounter. Invest in this area. Buy creams, deodorants, lotions, body sprays, perfumes, and other personal care products. Consult women's beauty experts. Little things like this can save lives and precious hearts.

8. You Must Master the Art of Communication: Communication is the lifeline of every human endeavor. It is the life of every relationship. In catching and keeping your man for life, this can be a great ally. But first, what is communication, and then, what do we mean by the art of communication? Art essentially means a practical skill, cunning, or profession. Communication is the passing and exchange of information, ideas etc. by means of speech, telecommunications (telephone), the media etc. So the art of communication talks about good communication skills, knowing how to talk.

Knowing the right words to say and how to convey them effectively. Sometimes it's not just what is said but how it is said. There are books you can read to learn how to communicate effectively. Most relationships fail due to a lack of good communication skills on the part of the woman. Men also have this problem, but this book is addressed to women. You must avoid the use of offensive and provocative language in your bid to communicate your feelings and ideas. One way to capture a man and take him is in knowing how to talk to him. Be gentle and kind. Use words that build him up. Don't tear him down. Use words like "Please", "thank you" "I am sorry", "I see your point". Use soft and disarming words to take the strong captive. The first thing a man notices in a woman after her looks is how she talks. All the beauty in this world will not save a woman who will not train her mouth to speak the right things. There are numerous free online courses available on effective communication and emotional intelligence in communication. Take advantage of those opportunities and refine your speech manner.

When not to speak:

i. When you are being spoken to: Listen and wait for your moment. Listen first so that you can learn what to respond to. People who can't listen make very poor communicators.

ii. When you are angry: Resist that urge to let him have a piece of your mind. That is not necessary. Learn to rule your emotions well by refusing to succumb to them. Let anger pass and speak when reason dawns.

iii. When you don't know: Don't claim to know what you don't know. Investigate before responding. Say what you know about, and when you don't know about it, hold your peace.

iv. When you are afraid – fear is also another emotion to watch. Sometimes fear will lead you to say something that can lead you into trouble. Fear excludes reason.

Don't be a talkative -

It is better to talk less than is necessary than to talk too much. A man can be easily put off by a woman who talks too much. The Bible says even a fool when he (or she) keeps quiet is esteemed to be wise. Proverbs17:28. Sometimes we communicate better when we don't communicate. Learn to use the amazing power of silence to your advantage. The Bible also urges us to be (i) quick to hear, (ii) slow to speak, and (iii) slow to get angry. James1:19.

Effective communication, therefore, must be the ability to know what to say, how to say it, and when to say it, and also when not to say anything at all. What makes some girls talk too much in the presence of people of the opposite sex? Excitement. Sometimes it is an inferiority complex, or simply a matter of charm. Whatever the reason, effort must be put into seeing that words don't become the problem. Choose your words. Consider it and decide whether it is suitable for the person. Speak to build up, encourage, praise, empower, and direct. Catch your man with words no man can resist. Speak to the king in him. Embellish him with words of affirmation. Tell him what no other person has ever told him about himself. Be artful. Be creative. Don't be his mother. Don't nag. Even when you have to correct, do it indirectly.

9. **You Must Be Generous and Kind Hearted:-** Generosity gives power. Unbelievable power. The Bible states that "every man is friend to him that giveth gifts" (Proverbs 19:6). People love those who love them. So you want to catch your man? Then you must have the heart of a queen. A giving and a kind heart. Nothing can be gained from being stingy and selfish. It repels favor. Open your heart, open your hand. One key Rebecca applied that qualified her to be Isaac's wife was her generosity. She was a giver. Abraham sent his servant to a far country to get a

wife for his son Isaac. When this servant got there, he prayed a prayer

"O Lord God of my Master Abraham.. behold I stand here by the well of water and the daughters of the men of the city come out to draw water: and let it come to pass, that the damsel to whom I shall say, let down the pitcher, I pray thee, that I may drink and she shall say, Drink and I will give thy camels drink also and let the same be she that thou hast appointed for thy servant Isaac and thereby shall I know that thou hast shown kindness unto my master." Genesis 24:12 – 14.

When Rebecca showed up, she did just that. She gave him water to drink, a total stranger, and she also gave water to all his camels. And they were many camels. Vs 15 – vs22. She was not only kind to the man; she was also kind to his animals! That is the heart of gold. A rare heart. One thing you must possess if you want to have a significant influence on people. Be given to hospitality. Always have a smile on your face. Be kind hearted. "Be not forgetful to entertain strangers: for thereby (or through it) some have entertained angels unawares." Hebrew 13:2. When it becomes your nature to give and to be kind and welcoming, you will not know when you show it to the man of your dreams or someone related to him. Don't just be beautiful, be generous. Love people. Help people. Always leave people with a smile on their faces. Soon word about your kindness spreads, and no one can resist you. Don't start life thinking about who will give you, start life thinking about what to give to help somebody. Be royal. Be merciful. Be a giver. You will catch so many men and have the luxury to choose among so many.

10. You Must Be Industrious: What does it mean to be industrious? It means to be energetic. Not lazy. To be hardworking. To be tireless. To persevere towards a task. In this present day, things have changed. It was once the practice that women would stay at home, have babies, and do nothing else. Marrying a wife then was more of marrying a liability. Hence, the fear among eligible men to hook up with a lady and take her to the altar. You hear them saying things like "Marriage? Who has money for that type of thing?.. I can't even think of it now..." This has changed. There is a revolution underway. Women are no longer relegated to the role of sitting idly while men go out to hunt. Now women have taken their destinies into their hands. Today, women are overrepresented in the corporate industry. Bankers, lawyers, doctors, professionals. Even in sports, we find women proving their mettle. We have women in politics, including senators, speakers of the House, governors, deputy governors, Director Generals of government agencies, and even Women presidents.

In describing the virtuous woman, Solomon paints an unusual picture of a woman who does not wait for others to give her. He paints a picture of an industrious woman. I am told that in the pride of lions, the female lions or lionesses do the hunting while the male lion lies around waiting for her to return with the prey. When she does, she brings the prey to the male lion, who takes his share (the lion's share) and leaves the rest for the lioness and her cubs. To be a true lioness, you must get off the dependent mode and start fighting for spoils. You must wake up and start doing your own hunting. Hear King Solomon "Who can find a virtuous woman? For her price is far above rubies" Proverbs 31:10. The word "virtuous" here is taken from a Hebrew word "Chayil". It comes from the word "force". It has to do with an army. Wealth, virtue, valor, strength, ability, activity, company, great forces, goods, host, might, power, riches, strength, strong, substance, valiant, worthy. So when the bible says *"He that findeth a wife findeth a good thing…"*. It is saying that she is hard to find. There are women everywhere, why is he still searching for her? She is very scarce. Once he finds her, see what the bible says *"the heart of her husband trusts in her confidently and relies on and believes in her securely, so that he has no lack of (honest) gain or need of (dishonest) spoil". Proverbs 31:11 (Amplified version)*

A virtuous woman is a forceful woman. An enterprising and proof–producing woman. She is rich, she is powerful. She is strong. She is a lioness. Her "pride" is safe and secure because of her. Read Proverbs 31:10 – 28. She will do him good and not evil all the days of her life. "She eateth not the bread of idleness" vs. 12 and vs. 27. She is an asset. An addition. A blessing to her man. To catch your man and keep him for life, make him want to own you by adding value to yourself. Don't agree to eat the bread of idleness. It is not safe. Gone are the days when people saw marriage as a way to escape poverty. Refuse to be a liability to any man. Complete your education, get a job. If you can't get one, create one. Put your hands to work. Learn a trade. Do something. Just refuse to be idle. Even when you are married, find a way to contribute to the household. This is indeed important. Yes, I know that some men want their wives to sit at home and do nothing. Don't agree to that. Use your female skills and persuade him to give you something to do. Make yourself an asset no man can afford to lose.

11. You Must Be Spiritual - To catch a man and keep him for life, you need to assume an uncommon form. You can't be a shallow person and maintain a lasting relationship. You need to go deeper than that. You need to be spiritual. What does it mean to be spiritual? A spiritual thing is that which is unearthly, that which is concerned with or affecting the spirit or soul. It has to do with that aspect of you that is not tangible or physical. It is being able to keep in touch with your inner self, your true self. It has to do with your walk with God. It means mere physical values do not drive you. It means you can see the unseen using the eyes of faith. It means you can understand the more profound, unspoken meaning of words and actions. It means you have the uncanny ability to perceive motives and intentions. You can feel the underlying reality behind a thing. You are not easily deceived. You don't fancy people for what they have and what they don't have, but for who they are. It means you can give good counsel. Godly counsel, not misleading people. It means you are stable. You are whole and secure. You are not seeking anything in any relationship; you are not in it for only what you can get; you are there because of what you can give. A spiritual person is different. They stand out in the crowd. They don't say what everyone says. They don't go where everyone goes. They don't wear what everyone wears. They are not under any form of pressure to perform. They are free. They have found God, and that is enough. Don't seek a relationship with any man when you have not yet found God. Only God can give you the love you need. Once you have found Him, you are whole, needing nothing. His words feed your soul. You don't need anyone to affirm or approve of you.

You have His approval, and that is enough. He makes you whole. When people come into your life, they find that you are who they were looking for; their genuine desire. Get close to God. Men are drawn like magnets to women who have an authentic walk with God. Don't seek men, seek God, and you cannot keep men away from you. See what God does to you: His presence in your life overshadows you and hides all your dark spots: Your Achilles heels, your ugliness. He makes you beautiful. He surrounds you with an aura of class. People can't help but respect and value you. He makes you wantable, desirable. Try Him.

12. YOU MUST BE WELL BEHAVED

You must possess a good character: Don't let beauty deceive you. The beautiful ones are not yet born. No matter how attractive you think you are, someone out there will soon appear and turn you into a thing of the past; history. You can't afford to build on beauty alone. You need a great character. You must be beautiful within and without. True beauty begins inside and reflects outside. *"Favor is deceitful and beauty is vain: but a woman that feareth God, she shall be praised"* Proverbs 31:30

It may shock you to know that not all men are attracted to beauty. Some are suspicious of it. What good is beauty if your behavior is horrible? When we say character, we mean a good reputation, being known for good behavior. Character is also defined as the inherent complex of attributes that determine a person's moral and ethical actions and reactions. It is said that the main objective of proper education is the formation of character. The Bible makes it clear that *"A good name is better than silver and gold" (Proverbs 22:1)*. Men are not only looking for beauty, but also good character. Integrity. Trust. Reliability. Honesty. Proverbs 11:22 *"As a jewel of gold in a swine's snout, so is a fair (beautiful) woman who is without discretion (character)."* Reputation is what you are known for; Character is who you really are.

If, for example, a lady is known to be promiscuous, yet she is beautiful, no man will want to get into any serious relationship with her. They may just want to have sex with her and dump her, because she cannot be trusted to be faithful to one man.

If a lady is known to steal, she has sticky fingers that seem to take things without being given; it can ruin things for her. No matter how small it is, if it is not yours and you take it without the owner's knowledge, honey, it is stealing.

If a woman is beautiful yet she lies, she will fabricate stories that never happened; she will get into relationships and get out of them without knowing why. Lying gives one impression of the liar; they cannot be trusted.

What about gossiping? That too is bad. A gossip is a dangerous person to get close to. They are relationship breakers. How do you know a gossip? Anyone who delights in telling you about other people's business is a gossip. One day, it will be your turn to be gossiped about. Shun such.

Again, a lady seriously seeking a lasting relationship with her man must be sure she is not going to be the cause of a breakup.

Laziness is another negative. You must fight against such. Do your work when you should do it. Avoid procrastination. Be diligent. Make yourself love work.

Another bad character trait ladies should guard against is covetousness, Greed, Avarice, and Love for material things. Never being content with what you have, always fixating on other people's things. This isn't very pleasant. It can spoil things for you. This is what produces other evil things like envy, jealousy, and lust for what is forbidden. Shun all these things.

Your beauty may bring men close to you, only for your bad character to send them away from you.

Avoid insulting and provocative words. Resist the urge to make fun of people. They may laugh with you now, but avoid you later. Let your words be seasoned with salt. Be gentle. Be meek. Be good. Let your external beauty attract them to your true beauty, the one within. "Whose adorning let it not be that outward adorning of plaiting the hair and wearing of gold, or of putting on of apparel. But let it be the hidden man of the heart, in that which is not corruptible, even the ornament of a meek and quiet spirit, which is in the sight of God of great price." 1Peter 3:3- 4

13. You Must Be Humble and Meek: - Nothing can be gained from pride. It is a favor–killer. Humility is the most valid form of power. A humble woman has tremendous power over people. To be humble means to be lowly. Yes, you must be industrious, self-sufficient, and able to take care of yourself, but you must balance that with humility. I know men who won't even dare to marry a woman because she is comfortable and self-reliant. They feel that such ladies will be challenging to control. Since they can pay their bills, they don't need a man to do anything for them, how can any man have the ability to guide them and restrain their excesses?, they argue. Humility is having power and still not using it. It is being a powerful person and yet agreeing to serve as a servant. It is being God, the Creator of the heaven and earth, and yet agreeing to die the death of a thief. Yes, humility is the greatest key to promotion. *"God resists the proud and gives grace to the humble." 1 Peter 5:5.* A proud woman will end up alone. No man wants to marry a woman he cannot manage. Be submissive and under control. Humble yourself and serve in the home just as he serves you too.. Make it your culture to esteem others better than you. Don't despise anybody. Only fools despise people based on their present circumstances. A wise person knows that a failure today can be a winner tomorrow. So he does not look down on anyone. He treats all men equally — with respect and dignity. Learn this. If you struggle with submitting to authority, it's time to change that now. It begins in the home. Submit to your father's authority. Obey him. Serve him. Your mother, too, and whosoever is your guardian. Submit and be humble. It increases your favor. If you have senior brothers in your house, serve them too. One day, someone will notice how humbly you treat your brothers and form a good opinion about you. Don't say "I will only humble myself to my husband….." that is not true. If you can't humble yourself to constituted authority in the home, in the school, in the church, in the workplace, you won't, even when married. Be known as a humble person. If you can submit yourself and serve people placed over you, it won't be difficult to submit to your own husband in marriage. Let me say this: humility can control even the mighty. Use it. Your submission is your truest power. Don't neglect it. Don't let your family background, wealth, or accomplishments make you arrogant. Stay low. Let people discover by themselves how much you are worth. Don't tell it. They will respect you more. Sometimes a high-classed unmarried lady needs to assume the form of a lower-class person to find her man. Look vulnerable and weak even when you are as strong as iron. Be like water, be formless, assume the shape of any vessel you find yourself. Be adaptable, and you will always win favor everywhere you go.

14. You Must Be Faithful: This means to be loyal and steadfast. It also means not having sexual relations with anyone except your husband or wife. A faithful person is steadfast in affection or allegiance. It also talks about fidelity. Faithful people are very hard to find. The Bible says so. "Most men will proclaim everyone his own goodness: but a faithful man (or woman) who can find? Proverbs 20:6. It also tells us what kind of end a faithful person should expect to have. "A faithful man (or woman) shall abound with blessings…" Proverbs 28:20. You must be a faithful person. One who is trustworthy, dependable, loyal, and steadfast. This is an important trait. Men will do anything for that one woman who will be faithful to them. Faithfulness means you will be there when you are needed. It means you don't have the habit of failing expectations. It means you can wait for him to go and return. It means your "yes" is your yes and your "no" is your no. It means you can't be involved in double-dating or cheating. It means you don't say "I love you" to everyone you meet. You don't get intimate with just anyone. It means you can be trusted to keep a secret. Proverbs 11:13. It means things committed to your hands cannot fail. It means you can wait for things to get better because they will. Be faithful. That is a scarce quality you can find in people nowadays. But if it can be found in you, you can keep a man.

15. **YOU MUST BE A LOVER**

You must learn how to be his lover: One thing men find hard to do without is a woman who is a lover. One who does not restrain herself from pouring her affections on her love. Her man. Who is a lover? She is a devotee. A fan. An admirer. An ardent follower, believer, and admirer of someone. A lover is simply one who loves. Love is like that web skillfully wound by the spider, which once a fly or any insect gets hooked to, finds it difficult to break free from. The more it tries to free itself from the web, the more it is webbed into the labyrinth of webs. Be a lover. Love is like that jar of honey a fly falls into. The more it tries to come out, the more it buries itself into it. It is useless to resist a true lover. To catch and keep, you must learn the art of love. I am not talking about sex here. Most times, sex becomes an escape route for the man: an easy way to get rid of you from his mind. Don't do that. Use love instead. Speak love into his head till he can't think of anything else but you. Call him all those sweet names. Mean it. Be his devotee. His fan. His best friend. His lover. Be for him a calm and soothing shade in a hot and harsh world. A place he will always want to return to, his way out of the harsh realities of life. Love him. The man needs to be loved. Pamper him. Pet him. Soothe his wounded ego with soft words of admiration, respect, and affection. Tell him words no other person has told him – about him. Talk to the king in him. Cheer him into victory. Sing his praises. Let him know you adore him. Point out his good qualities. His fine face. His sweet voice. His personality. Notice things about him nobody does. Feed him with your love till he won't need another. Once a man receives enough love from his lover, he becomes fulfilled and no longer finds any other woman attractive. It is unsatisfied men who seek love elsewhere. This goes to the married: Your husband is your number one priority. Make him that. Don't restrain yourself from showering all your love on him. Call him your hero, your heart, your baby, your lover, your soul, your life, your everything. You can conquer a man with love. He can't do without you. Always seek out better and more creative ways of loving him. This works wonders.

xvi. You must be a good Cook: You must know how to cook. Cooking is a powerful skill to acquire. There is power in cooking. People can't resist the smell and taste of good cooking. It opens doors into the heart of men. It is said that the way to a man's heart is through his stomach. That is to say, to win a man's heart, you must satisfy his stomach with good food. Cooking to me is an art: a form of expression. It is another way a woman can communicate with people. A sweet woman cooks sweet dishes. A disorganized woman cooks the same way. You are what you cook. Just like art, every man's work is a portrait of himself. You are your product. If your food is too salty and sour, it says a lot to people about you. When people eat a lady's dish, they are indirectly eating from the lady. To cook means to concoct. To prepare a meal by mixing ingredients. It is a form of invention. It is creativity at work. Take special care with your cooking. One major bond that keeps a man tied to his mother is her cooking. "Nothing tastes like mama makes it" you hear them say. That is a secret to work with. No person is born a good cook. Just like every other form of art, it is learned. So learn it. People have sold even their birthright because of a good meal. Ask Esau. For a morsel of porridge, he sold his birthright to Jacob, his brother. Genesis25:29-34

In the same way, Isaac could not bless Esau until he made him a dish he loved. Genesis 27:3-4 "that my soul may bless you before I die". Watch that word "my soul..." Good food can unlock the soul of a man and bring out all the treasures locked therein. How can something that enters the stomach affect the soul? That is the mystery behind good food. This is one secret some women who run restaurants and fast food joints know. They know the heart of a man is where his food is. So you find them being patronized by married men who have wives at home! Should this be so? I don't think so. Woman, arm yourself for war! Acquire the skill of creative cooking as one of your weapons. Be artful about it. Be methodical, be deliberate and calculated. Pour your creative abilities into it. Vow that no one will eat your meal and desire another. Learn new recipes every day. Be good at it. Catching and keeping your man for life has a lot to do with what you feed him. This is so important. It's not too late to start. You can start now. Buy a cookbook or have an expert train you in the tricks of the game. Good food has enough power even over the souls of men. Know this about men. There are four things a man does not play with:

i. He does not joke with his God

ii He does not joke with his work

iii He does not joke with his food

iv He does not joke with his sexual needs.

These four represent four areas of hunger in a man's life.

i. Hunger for God, to be at peace with God

ii Hunger for recognition and respect; through his work.

Iii Hunger for sex, – relationship, intimacy, satisfaction.

Iv Hunger for good food at the right time.

If you can't give him all four of them, do your best to give him good food. That is a good place to start. Sex comes after marriage, and that too must be served well and with the highest attention to creativity and detail. (This refers to the married). Work towards being skillful and unpredictable in everything you do.

THINGS WOMEN DO THAT DRIVE MEN CRAZY

Chapter Seven

MAJOR TURN OFFS

Things most men don't like in their women. Major turn-offs to avoid:

1. Most guys don't like a girl who can't speak correct English. A lady should be able to express herself accurately. Avoid bad grammar. Use your dictionary a lot. Learn a new word every day. Avoid bad spelling (especially in texts and letters).

2. Most guys don't like overweight women. Some do but most don't. What makes a lady overweight is relative. As a rule, looking shapeless and disproportional can be a major put-off. Adopt a new exercise habit. Maintain a trim and fit body. Love yourself, reduce your daily food portions, and exercise daily. You will notice some significant changes with time.

3. Many men prefer their partner not to be too thin. While being overweight is on one bad side, being too skinny is not good either. They want a woman with some "flesh" in the right places.

4. Most guys don't like a woman who talks too much. Communication is a very important life wire of every relationship. But over-communication can be a big put-off. Know when to speak up and when to remain silent.

5. Many guys prefer a girl who is not overly friendly with everyone. They often desire their partner to be exclusive and somewhat reserved. Once you're in a relationship with a man you love and who loves you, it's important to be mindful of how you

interact with other men. Be cautious and limit how you express affection, especially towards other guys. Showing respect for him is key.

6. Many men dislike it when a woman complains excessively. It's quite unpleasant. Avoid wearing a long face or acting as if the whole world is against you. Instead, try to look bright and happy. Even when you're facing difficult times, maintain a cheerful and non-complaining demeanor. This positive attitude is attractive. Constant complaining can drive a man crazy and may even push him away. Remember, there are people enduring much worse situations who can still smile and keep their struggles to themselves. You should strive to be one of those women, as they possess a special kind of strength.

7 Many men appreciate women who demonstrate a willingness to be understanding and open to guidance. This attitude often begins in the home and can influence future relationships. Reflecting on your response to authority figures, such as your parents, may provide insight into how you engage with others. While being assertive can be valuable, it's also important to strike a balance, as some men may prefer more accommodating partners. Showing respect for authority, being a good listener, and maintaining a willingness to learn can be beneficial. Additionally, cultivating emotional intelligence and managing your reactions—especially in challenging situations—can help preserve your reputation and foster positive interactions.

8 Additionally, the majority of men cannot stand a woman who lies. It's unwise to deceive others; always tell the truth. Honesty remains the best policy. Avoid lying, as it leads to complications when the truth eventually comes to light.

Other Turn-Offs

9. **Being Entitled**: Feeling that you are owed something simply because you are a woman can lead some ladies to make unreasonable demands of a man, and they may get angry when he is unable to meet them. If this describes you, it's important to stop and reflect. Remember that nobody owes you anything. Until you make a deposit in a relationship, you have no right to demand a withdrawal. Focus on adding value to a man's life, and he will feel indebted to you.

10. **Being Fake**: Pretending to be something you're not is a major turn-off. Men can easily see through a fake persona, and authenticity is highly respected. Be yourself and let others decide if they are interested in you. Authentic people are admired for their honesty—let your "yes" be genuine and your "no" clear.

11. **Being Rude**: Rudeness is a trait that nobody appreciates. It conveys arrogance and an unhealthy sense of self-importance. Always strive to be courteous and respectful to everyone you encounter, even strangers. You never know when you might need their support. Kindness costs nothing and goes a long way.

12. **Maintaining Connections with an Ex**: Many men do not want to be with a woman who hasn't moved on from her past relationships. This sentiment is likely mutual among women as well. If a lady is still hung up on her ex, she may not be ready for a new relationship. She needs time to heal and rediscover herself before entering the dating scene again. Many relationships are burdened by past hurts and experiences. Men tend to be possessive; they want to feel secure in knowing that their partner is thinking of them and no one else. The quickest way to lose a good man is by clinging to another man. Men generally do not share unless they are only looking for a casual fling.

UNDERSTANDING SEDUCTION

Chapter Eight

LAWS OF SEDUCTION

This is a very crucial matter. It is with great caution that I tread on this uncharted course. Why do I call it "uncharted"? This is because it is a very delicate subject. Seduction is a reality we must all confront squarely. It is either you are seducing or you are being seduced. For a woman desiring to catch her man and keep him for life, you must know all there is to know about this subject. Most times, it is people who don't know about it that fall prey to those who know it and use it. You hear of a sister complaining bitterly about another woman who "snatched her lover or husband". Why should a woman be alive and allow another woman like her to snatch her man? Is there anything in that other woman that she does not possess? Hardly. One may define a woman as one meal served in different dishes. There is nothing a woman has that another does not also have. God created all women the same. Understanding this subject, seduction, equips you to take what is yours and protect it from intruders.

WHAT IS SEDUCTION?

But first, we ask, what is not seduction? People have amusing ideas about seduction. That is why the subject remains taboo to a lot of well-meaning folks. Seduction is not about sex. If anything, sex has the power to kill seduction. It is difficult to maintain control over someone you are sexually involved with. It is the absence of sex that makes seduction a lethal weapon of absolute power. Seduction is not about exposing body parts to stir a man's sexuality. You must remember your body is not the only body he is seeing. Exposing vital body parts smacks of desperation, and it shows that one has lost control already. Seduction is clothed. It leaves everything to the imagination. The less he sees, the more he fantasizes about what it is like. Keep him dreaming.

Never reveal your assets to him. Don't show your breast, for instance, and wear dresses that leave nothing to the imagination. Granted, you will create a response, but that is not the kind of response you are trying to get. Don't make yourself cheap. Don't appear desperate and morally loose. Seduction is not physical. It is sexual energy that compels attraction. It is an invisible force. It's not the dress you wear but what the dress portrays about you. Seduction is what makes a woman stand out among women. It gives that larger–than–life appeal that presents you differently in the eye of the beholder. It is influence. Seduction is not dirty talking. It's not trying to show that "I am available..." Far from it. In this book, learn the truth about seduction. It is what you need to catch your man and keep him for life.

So, what is seduction? It is neither eroticism nor lewdness. It's not shaking your backside like a strip dancer and acting funny. Don't make the mistake of thinking that all men have the same taste. What then is seduction? Eroticism appeals to the animal nature in man. It stirs him sexually and releases a hormone in his body called Testosterone. Once his sexual passions take over his mind, all he is thinking about is taking you to bed so that he can get you off his mind. Seduction is not about appealing to the baser nature of man, the animal in man. It's about gaining complete control over his emotions, filling his mind with thoughts of you, and getting him to fall madly in love with you. Failure to seduce is at the base of all relationship failures.

In this chapter, I will show you, line upon line, how to carefully spin a web around your personality like a spider, waiting for your victim to be caught in it and never able to break free. The issue is that you need to get him madly in love with you and make him yours for life. It's easy…..

RULES OF THE GAME

Observe these rules.

1. Get him off your mind:

Seduction is compromised when one becomes emotionally attached to the target of seduction. Yes, he must have some level of impact on you, but you must not succumb to it. You can't play this game well if you are the overly emotional type. How do you get him off your mind? Focus your mind on other activities. Get your mind on other things. Get busy. Read a book. Go to work and really work! The less you think of him, the more power you will have.

Do not fall for his charms – at least not yet. You need a clear mind to be successful in this. To catch your man, he must not catch you first. Learn to deploy all those emotions to other purposes. At the onset of every relationship, use your head and keep your heart out of it until the ground is level, until he puts a ring on your finger.

The less a woman thinks about a man, the more he wants her. When I say not thinking about him, I am talking about not getting emotional or falling in love with him prematurely. The aim is not to fall in love with him. First, you must get him out of your mind. Think less of him. Create a distracting activity that can help you regain control of your emotions. See him less. Be objective. Be focused. Be deliberate. Fall in love, but not now. Love has a way of blocking out reason. It makes it difficult to break a relationship when it has gone wrong. You can't play this game of seduction until you master your emotions.

2. **Get Into His Mind:**

Fill his mind all day with thoughts of you. Get him to fall in love with you. The woman who has a man is the woman who has his mind. The one he can't get off his mind. The one he thinks about all day. Now, be very careful. That a man tells you that he is thinking of you does not mean he is actually thinking of you that much. It is a trick to take you off guard. Don't listen to his words, watch his actions. When a man is genuinely in love with a woman, it shows. There are things to look out for:

i. She is always in his thoughts

ii . He is always seeking opportunities for them to meet. He wants to be with her.

iii He talks about her with friends and close ones.

iv He is willing to make changes in his life to please her.

v. He is generous. What he does not give her is what he cannot give her. A man in love is a giver. Gifts, presents, tokens of love and affection. Nothing seems too much.

vi. He can't think of any other woman. No man can love two or more women the same way. It's practically impossible. Even if he keeps ten lovers, he will love one of them more than the others. Love is always singular, never plural. A man in love with a woman suddenly loses taste for others.

viii. He is very emotional. An emotional person is one in touch with their feelings. Emotions like anger, jealousy, pity, and joy are always present. Does he get angry when you don't show up as planned? Does he get jealous when he sees how you smile at others? Does he feel you are not giving him enough of yourself? Does he seem to want to possess you for himself? A man in love is highly emotional. He can't hide his feelings.

ix. Is he in a hurry to marry you? Once a man finds his true love, he will want to seal it at the altar. Be cautious of men who seem to be in no rush to make it official. True love can't wait!

x. Does he shed tears? Yes, I know. Men don't cry. They are superhuman beings from Mars. They have no feelings, and they are men! Yes, but love can turn a man into a crying baby. This is not a rule; it does happen. Love is the only force that can cause a man to shed tears. Tears of deep affection. Tears of devotion. Tears of love.

xi. Does he seem sensitive about your feelings? Does he notice the changes in your mood? Does he care about how you feel on the inside? Love makes a man sensitive. He is in touch with your feelings. Now, not all men may manifest all these above-listed traits, but they will manifest most of them.

Get him to think about you. How?

· Create unforgettable moments in his life.

· Speak words that spark his mind. Words that build him up. Words that speak to the king in him. Words that highlight his strengths and accomplishments. Words that make him feel better than he is.

· Leave traces of you around him. Bring him a gift that will always remind him of you – a wrist watch, cufflinks, shoes, perfumes, or wall paintings. Buy him the tools he needs to do his job. For a writer, a pen is essential; for a painter, a brush; for a businessperson, a diary to keep track of business contacts, etc. A wall clock. Little, inexpensive, but highly effective gifts.

· Remember his birthday and be the first to wish him a happy birthday. (Make it a duty to get him something for his birthday.) Most Men are emotional about their birthdays. That is the only day that belongs to them.

· Send him inspirational messages – words of motivation through texts, emails, Whatsapp messenger, and cards.

No man can forget such a woman. Don't allow him to forget you. Not even for a day. You don't have to be always around physically to achieve that; you can use other means. Most times, always being around may cause you to lose value in his eyes. The more you are seen, the less you are noticed. Create presence through absence. Let your works speak for you in your absence.

BASIC RULES OF THE GAME continued

3. Make him chase after you

The key to seduction is not to appear as the seducer but to appear as the one being seduced. You can make the hunted become the hunter. Women often wonder, "What do I do when I meet a guy I like who doesn't seem interested in me? How can I get him to be interested in me?" Well, that is what I deal with in this section. The tragedy of life is that while we are avoided by those we want, we are disturbed by people we don't like. How do we change the tide?

a. Determine the person you want. Choose the man you want to get.

b. Ensure he is not seriously engaged or married to someone else.

c. Study him. Find out everything there is to know about him — where he lives, where he works, who he hangs out with. Which church or group does he belong to, etc.

d. Strategize your next moves — Arrange for "chance" meetings. Make him notice you by appearing in the places you know he goes to. Pick up an interest in what he does. Join his group. All you need is an opportunity for him to see you. Once he notices you, 50% of your job is done.

e. Does he seem uninterested even after seeing you? Maybe not. You see, men can be shy. He may fancy you, but may not know how to approach you. Make it easy for him by establishing contact with him if he is a workmate in the same workplace, and pretend to approach him with a problem. Nothing seduces a man like the thought/prospect of helping a woman out of a problem.

From the moment the first contact is made, he will have determined how far this relationship will go (to himself).

f. Listen to his advice. Be visibly interested in what he has to say. Don't be fake about it. Listen, learn. Assume the posture of a willing student sucking up the knowledge of her master. Ask the right questions and return with feedback. Men can't resist the woman in need. So, create a need he can solve, and by doing so, get into his thoughts. The more he feels he is helping you, the more he sees you visibly improving because of his help, the more he likes you. Every teacher likes the student who learns fast. Give him the opportunity to contribute to your progress. It gives him a sense of control and self-worth. It also makes you look in his eyes as a poor, weak, vulnerable prey to catch. The weaker and vulnerable you appear, the more seductive you are. Weakness seduces the strong. If you don't have a need he can meet, then create one.

Ladies also ask questions like: **"Is it right for a sister interested in a guy to make the first move?"** That is to say, can a lady walk up to a guy and say, "I like you. Can we be friends?". Well, it is a little dicey. That might work, considering the scenario already created. If you are sure the guy likes you and is into you, you can make that move for him. Like I said, sometimes men are shy. I know a lady who walked up to a brother and said, "I like you. Marry me and I will do you good all your life..." and the brother did just that – he married her and today they are happy! Before making such moves, ensure that a level of relationship has been developed. Ensure you know him well enough to know how he would respond to that. This works when you have done your job well; you have made an impression in his life that he can't deny. You have him eating from your hands. He can't take offence at your boldness.

Once you know him that well, you can make that move. Desire is infectious. You can want someone so much that he is also affected by it and feels the same way, but once you are sure you have put your hooks on him and he is now yours, then withdraw. Act suddenly uninterested. First, stir his interest by telling him point blank how you feel about him, that action will take him off guard and soon you begin to dictate the flow of this affair. Once you have taken him, he is now hooked on you, withdraw… it is now his turn to chase. This brings me to the next step.

4. Tactical withdrawal:

It is now time to be scarce. It is time to put up your mood swings, to tell him you are busy. To seem suddenly uninterested in him. Doing this is how you regain your self-dignity—knowing that you stirred him and now he wants you. First, behave like he is everything to you and you can't live without him; next, show him your other side – your cold side. Let that be your vengeance for being forced to act first. Let him pay for what he put you through. Be tactical about this. Don't overdo it. Withdraw, respond, and then withdraw again. Keep him on tenterhooks. Keep him confused. Seduction thrives in confusion. Complexity is the power of seduction. What a man can't figure out he cannot control. Sometimes, pick up quarrels with him over nothing and observe him. If he is really into you, he will be on his knees begging you to forgive him for heaven knows what. Now you are in absolute control. You are now in the position to decide the outcome of this affair. The key is to be unpredictable. The more he can't understand you, the more seductive powers you have over him. This is when to get him to commit totally to you. Show no mercy, at least not now. From time to time, throw him some crumbs of affection and love, and suddenly stop.

This back and forth attitude is the only way to control a man. First, get him to fall in love with you by showing him much affection, and then withdraw. The rest will be up to him.

To be successful in this, you must master the art of measured emotions. You must be in total control of yourself. You must never give in to sex. Once you do that, your spell is broken. Keep your distance. Be near and far at the same time. Make yourself an adventure he will never forget. A goal he may never attain. A game he may never catch. Or maybe he will, who knows?

5. **Create competition:**

There is a principle that says that everyone wants what everyone wants. The more you are desired, the higher you are valued. You can move a prospect's hand by making him believe that you have many people desiring your hand in marriage (And I am sure you do). A man needs to know he is not the only one. It keeps him on his toes. I am not suggesting promiscuity, far from it. Nothing devalues a woman in the eyes of a man like promiscuity. Knowing that other men have had her brings her low in his eyes. Don't play that game. You can't win. I am talking about seduction. Creating desire: making him want you more. Keep a company of male friends, associates, colleagues, or simply admirers, suitors. People who also want you. Once he knows how much you are wanted, he will do everything in his power to wrest you from his perceived rivals. Make yourself a trophy he wants to win at all costs. The value of a thing is not in the thing but in who it was taken from. Have the person you want to catch in mind and use others to put pressure on them to act.

i. He will treat you with value

ii . He will be in his best behavior.

iii He will lavish you with gifts to compete with what others are doing for you.

iv. He will rush you to the altar before someone else does.

Sometimes, pretend you are confused about who you want. Feign affection for others. Make him believe you are doing him a favor by agreeing to marry him. This is the best way to tame any man. He will "gratefully" marry you. On the other hand, if other ladies like you also desire your man and you seem to be pressured by this – don't be. Withdraw. Don't try to compete with them. Give him space to choose. Just be sure you are doing for him what none of them can do for him. How do you do that?, Find out what he is getting from them and give him more or less than that. Do they all seem to like him too much and want to possess him, and now you seem to be losing out? It's easy, withdraw and appear at strategic moments. Study his moments and invade him when he is most vulnerable. Don't seem to fall for his charms. You are not impressed. Tell him you are ready to walk out, and show it. Show him he can't have you and anyone else. Let him know you know your worth. Don't beg or cheapen yourself. Just withdraw, soon he will leave the others and come for you. Sometimes absence speaks louder than presence.

Is he already yours, but others are trying to take him from you? Simple. I will deal with this in the next chapter

TAKE BACK YOUR MAN!

Chapter Nine

DEALING WITH THE COMPETITION

Get rid of the people trying to steal your man

FIRST THINGS FIRST

a. You Must Evaluate the Situation: There are battles to fight and battles to avoid. Jesus in His parable advised us to sit down and count the cost of the proposed battle before embarking on it. There is no point fighting a battle you can't win. Luke 14:28. Evaluate the situation: Is he truly committed to you? Is his heart entirely devoted to you? Or does he seem confused about who he wants? Does he seem to be managing or patronizing you? "Yes, I love you," he says, "but…".

If you are not sure of him, there is no point in fighting for him. The battle is already lost. If he is not sincere about his commitment to you, you can't afford to build on that. It is a risk. In every relationship breakup, the most important thing is who ends it. It is usually the other person, the one dumped, who suffers the rejection and depression that follows. Don't wait until he tells you it is over. Act first: dump him! That is the only way you will gain back all the energy you lost in the affair. At least when you walk away, you will tell yourself, "I ended it". It gives you the power to rebound again. This also means that you won't have to entertain any inferiority complex or feelings of rejection in your mind. Ending a bad relationship gives you the psychological power to survive the breakup. It also gives you the strength to start all over again. If your competitors seem to be having an upper hand in his life, walk away. That may be the thing that will jolt him back to reality. Some men can't bear to be dumped or rejected. It will wake him up to the fact that he is not all that charming. It humbles him. Once you are sure that you will ultimately lose, leave with your pride and your dignity. Call off the engagement. I know it may not be easy, but it is the best thing to do under the circumstances. To deal with the competition, don't seem to compete at all. What is yours is yours. Period.

In evaluating the situation, find out these:

i. Is the competitor physically better than you are in his eyes? Is she more beautiful? Does she possess qualities you don't have? Qualities you've seen him admire in other ladies? Walk away. Even if he eventually marries you, he will still give his heart to "Rachael". This is the reason for a lot of extramarital affairs. Let him go now. Yours will come.

ii. Has he made some commitments to this competition? Has he pledged marriage to her before meeting you? Has he gone as far as meeting her parents? Do your investigations.

iii. Is she pregnant for him? Does she have children for him? Have they gone very far, and now he wants to abandon her for you? He will do the same to you when he meets another person better than you.

iv. Is he worth the trouble? Is he everything you want? Is he trustworthy? Has he shown evidence of total devotion to you? Do you both agree on major issues? Is he your type of man? Do you perceive that you are destined to be together forever? Does he share the same sentiments and values as you? Is he yours? Then fight for him!

To deal with the competition, having established the points we mentioned, you are ready to fight a battle you know you have won, but first, who is this competition? In what form do they manifest? Should we worry about them?

This is the whole essence of this book. You must be aware that you are not the only one interested in this man that you want. There are others out there who will do everything in their power to have him. Enemies of purpose who love to reap where they did not sow. Daughters of Jezebel. Hawks perched around, looking for whom to snatch. You see them everywhere in the workplaces, in the schools, on the streets, in the neighborhood, and even in the church! They are everywhere, looking for whom to devour. You must protect your man from them. You must know how to eliminate them and destroy their influence. Some of them you know, some you don't know. They are women without virtue and discretion, not seeking their own; instead, they take special joy in stealing from others.

The good news is that they are neither invincible nor infallible. They are mere mortals, women like you who are not better than you. You can overcome them. I will show you how.

First of all, the psychological disposition of a husband or lover snatcher is one to be pitied. They don't believe in themselves. They don't think they have what it takes to get their own man. They suffer from low self esteem. They have a second class mentality. Instead of believing in God for their own man, they prefer to stoop so low as to snatch another person's love. Dealing with them with this understanding makes it cheap to handle them. They are inferior to you. They are not better than you; you are better than them. You must win the psychological warfare here. Don't see it the wrong way – which is that he is interested in them because they are better than you. That is the wrong way to see it. He is showing interest in them because he is a man. It has nothing to do with not loving you. You can get him back.

Now let me talk to the married and those engaged to marry. The keys I will lay forth here will be helpful to you.

Key 1: **Analyze Your Competitors:**

You cannot compete against a rival you don't know or understand. Study the competition. What is it in this rival that turns him on or stimulates his interest in them? What does he like in them? Are these qualities you can acquire? Is it a physical quality you can get? Study them. Take notes. Are these qualities you can compete against or acquire?

Key 2. **Emulate (mimic) the Competition:**

To mimic simply means to mirror. To imitate. Nothing frustrates the opposition, like imitation. It leaves them powerless and useless. They pride themselves in being able to offer what you cannot offer, in being different from you. You deny them that boast by mimicking them. Let the man turn and see them in you. Copy their every move. I am not referring to a particular competition. The trick is to view every woman around as a potential competition. Mimic them. It frustrates them. If you are exactly like them, how can they outclass you? Ensure that you accomplish this while staying true to your identity.

iii. **Innovate:**

While mimic means to do what the opposition or competition does, innovation means to do what they cannot do. Embrace the essence of everyone around you while also striving to reach your full potential. Stay one step ahead. Make changes, introduce new ideas, and keep your mind active. Soon, everyone will follow the trend you set. Outpace the competition by first imitating them and then surpassing them through innovation. Use your advantage well. You are the one he is committed to. Use that office well. Be creative.

iv. **Improve on yourself:**

Self-improvement is an ongoing process. Physically – strive always to appear elegant and sexy. Man is a visual creature. He is controlled by what he sees. Give him something to see. Work out to keep fit. Strive to look better than your best. Mentally – strive to know more. Move up intellectually. Grow with him. Keep improving. We have taken pains to talk about some of these things in previous chapters. Perhaps you should reread this book.

v. **Use your sexuality:**

You are a woman. Be a woman. Seduction is about being sexy and desirable – Period! The day you begin to lose your sexual appeal, you start to lose. To the married, I say, use sex constructively. Give him something to do. Let him exhaust all his wild oats on you. Lure him to sex at odd hours. Pay him a surprise visit at his workplace, wearing next to nothing (that is, if he has his own office), let him meet you at home walking practically nude with a boot and a tie, pretending to be his secretary, or one naughty thing. Use your imagination. Sex must not be dry and predictable – make him do it in unusual places – in the kitchen, in the bathroom, in the car, under the stairs. Give him sexual encounters, and he will be thinking about them all day. Be sexy. Break every rule and get down with it. Spice the room with sweet perfumes. Light a candle and play a romantic song in the background. (It doesn't have to be a Christian song!). Do crazy things together. Check into a hotel and have some crazy fun with him there. Fulfill all his sexual fantasies. Learn the art of lovemaking. It is an art. Read books on it. Practice with each other on any new tricks. This is so crucial. Give him an experience he can't forget. The competition (if any) will look for someone else to seduce because you are a master in the game. Wear what he wants you to wear. If he wants trousers, wear trousers for him. If he wants micro mini, wear it for him (at home). Keep him feasting his eyes on your beauty all day. Match seduction with seduction. Use your sexuality to the maximum. Give him what he wants, when he wants it, where he wants it, how he wants it… I don't know. Talking about this is getting to me now. My body is reacting funny just saying these things. I need to be with my wife now. Excuse me…………….

Alright, let's continue from where we stopped. Where were we?

ELIMINATE THE COMPETITION

Key 1. **Eliminate the competition**

Sometimes it is best to eliminate any perceived threat. Get rid of the person or persons. If you think a female secretary is becoming an unnecessary temptation to your man, ask him to replace her with a more reliable person, or a male secretary. Is it a housemaid or female attendant? Get rid of her. Is it your close friend who is becoming "too close" to him these days? Get rid of her. This is what Sarah did. When Hagar began to act like she was something, she got rid of her. Genesis 21:9-14. Do the same. Be alert to notice any wrong movements and take action swiftly. Protect your man.

Key 2. **Isolate your man from others**

The greatest law of seduction is isolation. To keep him under your influence, you must seek to remove him from "hostile" environments. Seduction works best in your own environment. Don't talk to him with his friends around him. Call him out and say what you want to say. He will listen to you more when you're alone with him than when people are around. Always seek to be alone together with him. Never criticize him in public. Go out together on a date and spend quality time together. The more you stay together, the stronger the bond. Take a long vacation together.

Key 3. **Avoid driving him away with your mood swings.**

Don't allow yourself to take offence at every wrong behavior. Learn how to smile even when you want to explode. Sometimes it's good to be moody and seem sad to attract his attention and maybe get pampered; it's all good. But don't overdo it. If he feels locked out of you because of your moodiness, you may drive him out to seek people who will smile with him, and there are many of them. Learn to be forgiving and tolerant. Don't drive him farther away, let it go. Forgive and forget. Provide him with a refuge from the challenges of life. Always make sure to greet him with a smile and a warm embrace when he returns from work. And most importantly, don't be a bag of complaints. Avoid the tendency to wear a long, sorrowful face, like the world is on your shoulder. Don't do it. Smile. Be happy. Look happy. Don't turn every meeting into another opportunity to complain about your needs and wants. Smile. Make him love your company. Don't give room to the enemy. Ephesians 4:27

Key 4. **Ignore the competition**

The less you make them think they are a threat to you, the more you confuse them. Always seem to be secure and settled in your relationship. Never betray any sign of problem in your relationship or marriage. Sometimes these snatchers want to see a little sign in your face that you are not happy, that gives them the green light to sweep in. Don't make them an issue. If you are doing everything I have said in this book, they can never be a problem to you. So ignore them. Smile when you meet them. Confrontation and loss of temper betray nothing but a woman who has lost out. You will be giving them what they want. Always speak well of your husband (or fiancée). Speak well of your union. Don't give room to gossips and housebreakers. Shun them. You are in charge.

Key 5. **Befriend the competition**

It is a known adage that says "keep your friends close, keep your enemies closer." There is a lot of wisdom in that. When you befriend the competition, you confuse and weaken them. They don't know what you are up to. Once you notice a female getting close and friendly with your man, sweep in to get close to her too. The more friendly you get with them, the more difficult it will be for them to flirt with your man. Shower them with love, buy their loyalty. Get into their skins. Soon it becomes easier for you to monitor them. Don't antagonize them, make them your allies and one day, they may be the ones helping to keep an eye on your man. If you can't get rid of them, get into them.

Key 6. **Pray**

This is the greatest key to catching your man and keeping him for life. Why pray? God holds the heart of every man in his hand. He created man, and He only can control and influence him. Prayer is taking sides with God to positively impact the man He made.

When you seek God and his kingdom, he makes everything obey you. Put God first, and no man will prove a problem to you. Prayer exerts God's influence in the heart of men, causing them to turn from their ways to the ways of God. This is why, if you are not yet married, seek to marry a godly man- a child of God. One who fears God. Such men will never give you problems. Are you already married to one who knows not God? Don't lose heart, for with God all things are possible. Trust Him and He will save that soul through your prayers. Prayer is the greatest weapon. By it, you catch your dream man, and by it, you keep him for life.

Be specific in your prayers. (For those sisters still searching for their man)

Ask God exactly what you want. Get a piece of paper and write exactly the kind of man you want. Describe him in detail – height, weight, complexion, profession, personality, etc. A young lady came to me seeking help, and I told her to do what I said now. She wrote everything about him on a piece of paper and stuck it on a wall in her room, and kept praying and thanking God for her dream man. You know what? Three months later that man manifested! Exactly as she desired. Today they are happily married and they live in London with their kids. God gives us exactly what we want. There is no point in desiring what belongs to another woman; instead, go to God in prayer, and He will give you what you want. Ask in Faith, believing Mark 11:23, 24, Matthew 17:21; 21: 21 – 23, James 1:5

Ask in the name of Jesus – John 14:13; 16:23- 24.

Ask, keep asking – Luke 18: 1- 8, don't give up asking.

Ask specifically: Mark 11:24 – say what you want.

Ask without a double mind- James 1:6 – 8

Be sure to confess all known sins and repent of it. God does not hear sinners (John 9:31, Psalm 66:18). Ask for His mercy and forgiveness for every mistake you have made. His blood washes away all your sins. I see God opening a new door of favor to you in the name of Jesus. Receive the man of your dreams and keep him for life. Peace! Give thanks to God for answered prayers.

WHAT THE SECUCTRESS KNOWS ABOUT MEN

Chapter Ten

THE SECRETS OF THE SEDUCTRESS

The things that seduce men.

As a bonus chapter, I will discuss the secret of the seductress. What is her trade secret? Why do men want her? What is it that they see in her? What is that magic she has that gives her such control over even the mighty? You find one lady waiting for years, with no serious person coming to her for marriage or even dating, while the other lady controls up to five men at the same time. She even has the luxury of dumping whoever she ceases to need and getting another to replace him. What is it about this woman that every man wants to be close to? Even the married men. Can a man be so controlled? Are there hidden secrets we can extract from her?

In this chapter, I will attempt to point out some of the secret things about the seductress. To begin with, we will study the book of Proverbs. We will see through the eyes of Solomon what he has to say about the seductress: her style, method and secrets. As a woman seeking to catch your man and keep him for life, you must be equipped with this knowledge so that you can counter the operations of this woman, the seductress. We will start with Proverbs 5: 1- 3 *"my son, attend unto my wisdom and hearken your ear to my understanding: for the lips of a strange woman drop as an honeycomb and her mouth is smoother than oil."*

She knows the power of words, sweet words. Smooth words; soothing words. Words that charm and seduce. She knows how to talk to a man. She flatters with her mouth. Flattering is her game. She knows what the man wants to hear and she gives it to him. Her words are as smooth as oil and sweet as honey. What does this mean? Oil and honey are two elements mentioned here. Oil is known for its smoothness and softness. When oil is rubbed on a hard surface, it softens and smoothens it. It dissolves every form of friction and resistance. For example, when a metal object is lubricated with oil, it runs smoothly and without wear and tear. Oil cannot be resisted. It enters places you can never believe. There is no known resistance to its penetrative power. The seductress knows the power of words. She coats her words with oil. She avoids hurtful and offensive language. She says only what he wants to hear, even if it kills him. Before we continue, I will highlight the points I got from studying this seductress Solomon speaks of:

i. Proverbs 5:3 – **Her lips are sweet as honey** and her mouth is smoother than oil: She uses sweet and non – non-threatening, smooth words to persuade her victims. She paints a picture of perfect bliss, sexual utopia and utmost pleasure for him, only to get his soul.

ii. Proverbs 5:6 – Her ways are moveable: you cannot know what she will do next. She is highly adaptive and incurably changeable. She is unpredictable. Always fashioning her skills to meet the diversity of every new catch. You cannot rely on her. She belongs to no man. She is a mystery. The day a man can control her is the day she dies. She is movable.

iii. Proverbs 5:8 – **She has a house:** A place she operates from. An environment she has created for relaxation. A place a man can feel free to stay with her. She makes it easier for her victim by providing a place for their escapades. Most men who consider the thought of cheating give up the idea because of the question of where to go and do it. She solves this problem by getting a place. She is prepared for him. She knows the obstacles that may stand in the way, and she gets rid of them. She is proactive.

iv. Proverbs 5:8, 9, 10 – **For her vanity, she will rob the man of his honor, his years.** She is thinking about a relationship that will run into years. She is not thinking short-term. You hear of extramarital affairs that go on for 20 years or more. She can keep a man for that long without him wanting to break from her. She also robs him of his wealth. You see a man with a family and children, preferring instead to spend his wealth maintaining that little mistress somewhere. There is a reason why he is working so hard, making so much money, and yet can't show for it. He is spending it on her! In exchange for pleasure, a man will give his wealth. The seductress knows this, and she sees to it. She also takes all of the man's labor. She makes him work his nails out, and for what? One more night of ecstasy. She knows the little fantasies that swim inside a man's head; she knows a man can give anything just for more pleasure. She gets him addicted to her pleasure. He can't have enough of her. So he works, toils only for her to take it all.

Instead of getting angry with her, why don't we ask what she is doing to get all this attention and favors? Some easily conclude that she uses a charm on him; she is diabolical. I agree, but I believe that such spells can be broken. Superior knowledge can destroy any charm. Besides, there is no type of charm or spell that prayer cannot break. Just know your place in God and your right as a believer. The seductress is not a shallow, stupid over-sexed little thing. She is a calculated, strategizing, and powerful huntress. She knows what she wants, and she will do anything to get it.

Let's study her more.

v. Proverbs 6:24 – **She is a flatterer.** She speaks sweet, smooth words to catch her victim. Let's talk a little about words. Seduction begins and ends in words. Most men resent women who talk in ways that offend their ego and pride. They want to be spoken to as though they have no fault. The less you confront a man with his fault, the better. Even when he knows you are right, he will seethe with offence and resentment. Men want to be pampered. To be treated like perfect little creatures (they are not). To be made to feel a sense of vindication, justification, and self-acceptance. He has all the criticism he needs coming from his boss, his rivals, parents, and sometimes from his trusted friends. He doesn't need another mirror showing him his "ugly and worthless self". Not at home. He needs a mirror that opens to a world of fantasy: a trip away from reality. He wants to hear words no one has ever told him, smooth and non–offending words. Sweet words. Ego-healing and soothing words. That is what he needs. The seductress knows this and showers him with these flowery words. She understands the power of poetry and can compose words that sweep him off his feet. Many women have chased their husbands away with words. Offensive words, nagging words. True sometimes, but lacking in skill, delivery, and tact. If you won't talk to him the way he wants to be spoken to, soon he will find someone who will. The seductress is a master flatterer.

To flatter means (**chelgach**) in Hebrew –this means smoothness, slippery places. Sometimes a man wants to be flattered. He may know you are flattering him, yet he is enjoying it. He wants to be told he is doing the best he can. He wants to be told: there is no one like him, he is the best thing that ever happened since…., he is handsome, he is good in bed (for the married) – nothing kills a man's sexuality like talking down his sexual prowess. Or telling him he is not good enough, or that his manhood (penis) is small etc. This is unforgivable.

Tell him sweet things about himself and why you love him. You are a woman. Be a woman! Men don't expect women to be rough and hard and annoying; they want women to be soft, smooth, and sweet. The seductress takes many victims because she is a master of smoothness. Isn't it a wonder that he prefers to spend all his wealth, years, and labor on her? There is a way to talk to a man and he will hand over his cheque book to you, signed, asking you to fill in anything. Use smoothness. I am not saying you cannot tell him the truth, especially when it saves his life, but you can do it with smoothness. Use soft, appealing words. Be selective. Be smooth. Be a Woman.

vi. Proverbs 6:25 – **She is lusty and seductive:** She knows a man will die to see her beautiful body. She crafts her dressing in such a way that evokes lust and desire in a man. She shows a little here and a little there. She covers but does not cover all. She leaves him dreaming and wondering what she looks like without those clothes. Now, her power is her clothing. That is what makes her beauty sexy and appealing. She must keep him guessing and wondering by revealing next to nothing. Once he sees her nude, her mystery is broken. So she continues to evade his advances. Coming close but not staying close, and showing him something of her body that sets his mind on fire with passion and lust. Lust is her weapon. Creating lust is her aim. She knows that once a man falls under the power of lust, he becomes an enslaved person to be ordered about and controlled. So she reveals a little flesh, supple soft skin, not too covered, not too revealing. All these are deliberately targeted at her victim. Lust is her game. Her body is her weapon.

MORE ON THE SEDUCTRESS

vii. Proverbs 6:25 " *Neither let her take thee with her eyelids…..* "
The eye of the seductress: Her eyes are full of contrasting signals. While her lips speak of virtue and goodness, her eyes betray a different expression. She speaks with her eyes. She says volumes with a short glance. Her victims are enchanted and held captive by the power of her seductive gaze. There is a spirit in her eyes that seems to draw men into her orbit. She has mastered the art of looking. Her eyes seem to bore into one's soul, holding every response captive to her hypnotic gaze. When you catch her staring, she blushes, putting up that innocent naïve expression that puts you into confusion—her eyes. No wonder Solomon exclaimed, *"Turn away thine eyes from me, for they have overcome me"* **Songs of Solomon**. She takes men with a look. A look that says *"I am available….. I will give you the experience of your life…….. I want you…"* Eyes that speak. To protect himself, a man best not look into those eyes.

vii.   Proverbs **6:26** *"And the adulteress will hunt for the precious life"*

She is a hunter: A huntress. A hunter chases after prey. He sets traps, baits, and snares to entrap his target. This woman does not sit around and wait to be hunted; she takes the initiative to go out and get her prey. She is dangerous. She knows where to meet him. She knows what he wants, and she waits for his most vulnerable moment to sweep in for the kill. She also knows that sometimes men want to be hunted and caught like they were some wild animal, needing to be tamed. She knows man's vanity and positions herself to supply it.

A hunter is a person who searches for something, like a treasure hunter. She is the hunter, and who is she hunting for? *The precious life.*

The word *"hunt"* is derived from the Hebrew word "*Tsuwd*". It means to hunt eagerly or keenly. It also means to chase. She is on the chase for good men. She follows them around, keeping track of their movements and never leaving him out of her sight.

The word *"precious"* here is taken from a Hebrew word, *"Yaqar"*. It means: valuable, priced, weighty, precious, rare, and splendid:

(a) Precious
(i) Costly
(ii) Precious, highly valued
(iii) Precious stones or jewels
(b) Rare
(c) Glorious, splendid
(d) Weighty, influential, costly, honorable, excellent, reputation.

This woman is not looking for just any man. She is looking for powerful men. Influential men. Men of honor. Great men. Men of great value. She is attracted to power. This is not just about romance, it's about power. She wants power, and to get it, she needs to capture the powerful. The higher the profile, the more attraction he holds for her. She has no time for nonentities. She wants power, and to get it, she must hunt for the powerful; she stalks his every move and finds a way of getting him to notice her. She must get him at all costs. This is why men should be cautious about whom they open up to. With whom they get intimate without their wives knowing. These people are gold diggers, looking to reap where they did not sow. Hunters of big fish. The more powerful a man becomes, the more cautious he must be because out there is a hunter seeking opportunity to catch him and own him. But let's look at this the other way. Why should the seductress have all the powerful men, while our sisters agree to settle with just anybody? The biblical Esther packaged herself so well because she was not going to settle for just any man. The king was her target, and she got him; she became his queen. You must not take what is offered to you. You must know what (or who) you want, and you must go for it. If the devil has sent his daughters to go and hunt good men to destroy them, then we must equip and send our daughters, God's handmaidens, to hunt and capture good men for His purpose. I believe that is why you are reading this book. To be equipped for this end-time battle for the souls of men, good men. God's men.

In hunting, you must apply the following rules:

(i) You must never let the prey out of your sight.

(ii) You must not let the prey know he is being hunted.

(iii) You must know the right trap to set.

(iv) You must know when to strike.

(v) You must strive to look like the prey. Adapt to his world.

The seductress is a hunter. She targets the men of power. Men of influence. Men of great value. She wants a part of that power, and to get it, she goes for those who have it. She has eyes for good men, precious and rare men. Men who carry a lot of weight. Men that people value and honor. Godly men. Men of purpose and reputation. These are her targets. Why must we let her get them all?

ix. **Proverbs 7:10** – "*and behold there met him a woman with the attire of a harlot, and subtle of heart*". This simple young man strayed into her territory. The prey had just found its way into the lion's den. Seduction works best in your territory. While he was straying into an unknown area, the woman met him. This woman was waiting for him to stray into her area. She was ready for him. He was her game, and she was the hunter. She knew men. She knew a man could be seduced by:

a. Getting him into your territory **(for men: watch out for those ladies that keep inviting you to come and see them in their house or their friend's house. Flee!)**

b. Taking the initiative: - Our society frowns on women who take the initiative. To them, it makes a woman appear loose and desperate. To an extent, this is true. Just like in any game, there are rules. But what do you do when your opponent seems not to be playing by the rules? What do you do when, while you are trying to abide by regulations, someone else wins by breaking the rules?

The rules of battle on the battlefield must be highly adaptive and flexible, Relative to the fight at hand. With the good, show yourself good, but with the lawless, show yourself as lawless while keeping the law of Christ. **1Corint.9:21**, what am I trying to say? Where did the Bible say a woman cannot approach a man she desires? I can't see it anywhere. When it says **"He that findeth a wife, findeth a good thing,"** it does not say a woman cannot find a man. After all in **Proverbs20:6,** He asks a question,

"a faithful man who can find?"

 Meaning that we are to look for faithful men. Just as a man should seek a virtuous woman as a wife, a woman should seek a faithful man. You know the funny thing? If good women don't learn how to search for and catch their men, strangers will. The seductress understands that sometimes a man may want her but lack the courage to approach her. So she makes it easy for him; she takes the initiative. She does what you are not willing to do, and she gets men cheaply.

It's time to awaken the daughters of Zion to the warfare of these contemporary times we are in. If he won't come to you, find a way to bring him to you or lure him into your territory. Man is constantly straying, looking for someone to catch him. May the good woman catch him first.

c. The third thing she does is that she appears in the dress of a harlot. Notice that the Bible does not call her a harlot. It calls her a woman. A harlot is a paid sex worker. A prostitute. The word *Harlot* here is taken from the Hebrew word *Zanah* – it means a whore. A prostitute. A fornicator. An unfaithful woman. An adulteress. A cult prostitute. To be wanton. This woman is not a harlot. But she knows something about some men. Some men like harlots. Men are seduced by women who have no problems giving themselves for sex. Yes, he may like the well-behaved, virtuous, good woman sometimes, but the other times he wants her to be naughty and crazy. She, a respectable, married woman, decided to appear to this catch of hers, not as a woman but as a harlot who seduced the man. He wants a mixture of virtue and villainy; of the maid and the mistress; of the good and the unbelievable. He likes a mystery. Once something is common and ordinary, he soon loses taste for it. He wants a little adventure with a strange woman. You can be the adventure he's looking for if you know how to combine the good girl with the "bad" girl. Wives should learn not just how to be good and gracious and legitimate, but also learn to be their husbands' sex liaison—one who caters to their unspeakable needs. One thing the seductress knows: *a sexually satisfied man is easy to keep.* He will keep coming back for more. So she adopts the form of a harlot. She knows man's vanity. He craves the forbidden flesh. So she makes it easy for him.

Refuse to be ordinary and predictable; it will bore him. Be creative. Be ready to be anything he wants you to be for him. Watch this woman. If she appeared in the form of who she was – a woman, probably the man wouldn't have fancied her. So she transformed herself into what he was looking for. She knew that man is visual – he is controlled by what he sees. To him, image is power. So she gets a costume. She becomes what he wants and cheaply takes him captive.

Question:

Should a woman become a harlot to catch her man?

Far from it. You don't have to be a harlot to dress like one. Be ready to be anything he wants you to be without losing your true identity. Let me make this point very clear: when I say some men like harlots, I don't mean they want them or that they would like to go to them. No. I mean that there is something about her attire that gets men. She seems to know the deep secrets of men and can become that for him. They want their women to be as hot as any woman out there. He wants his woman to be his harlot. A harlot knows the needs of a man and is willing to give them to him. She is very submissive to him and does not question him. She is naughty and can keep a man glued to her by constantly coming out with something different. She is a man keeper. She does not act as if she is trying to control him, even though she is in control. She gives him the impression that he is free to walk in and walk out. Eventually, even when he is free to walk out, he doesn't because she sets him free.

The best way to take people captive is to set them free.

Incorporate this in your operation and see how cheaply he will fall madly in love with you. To catch a man, set him free. **A man will give his soul to the woman who allows him to keep his**

freedom. I am certainly not referring to unfaithfulness on the man's part here, nor am I endorsing it. Far be that from me. No man is free to be unfaithful to his wife or betrothed. I am talking about being free enough to express one's deepest desires and wants without feeling ashamed or betrayed—freedom to be one's true self before the one they love.

d. The fourth thing the Bible says about this woman is that she is subtle of heart. She can hide her true feelings with misleading words and actions. She is cold and calculating. The word *"subtle"* here is taken from a Hebrew word *"Natsar"* – to guard; watch, watch over, keep. To guard, keep secret. To be kept close; to be blockaded; to be hidden. Her heart is full of guarded secrets. She never reveals her true intention in her words or actions. She is careful not to let her heart get in the way of her mind. She appears like a harlot, but she is not a harlot. She conceals her true identity. What she wears is not who she is. She can adapt to any environment and play along, while in her heart, she maintains her self–possession. She may tell a man anything he wants to hear and act the same way to win his heart. No man can lay claim to possessing the secret of a woman's heart. She can become anything you want her to be without losing herself in the process. She is subtle. Don't believe a word she says. She can make love to a man in one moment and turn and stab him to death in the next moment. She can make him feel so at home with her, washing his feet, massaging his back, pouring soothing oil on his tense nerves, and speaking sweet words into his ears, loving him to a state of absolute self-abandonment. She feeds him with her choicest milk and uses her finger to caress his head. He closes his eyes and gives himself over to his wildest ecstasy. And while he is relaxed and comforted in the embrace of a woman, she grabs a peg and a hammer and with one brutal strike pins his head to the ground with his blood shooting out of his brain–dead. (Reference to Jael in **Judges 4:18 – 21)**
It is because of this rare ability that the seductress appears to be unstoppable and irresistible. She studies the man, finds out his weakness, his secret passions, his unfulfilled dreams, and his

sexual fantasies, and takes the form of the woman who meets these needs while still maintaining her inward intentions. She gets him cheaply. She can mirror all the dark secrets of the man. She conceals her true identity until the right moment, then transforms into any form she desires, as long as it serves her purpose..

THIS WOMAN MEANS BUSINESS!

Chapter Eleven

STRATEGIES OF THE SEDUCTRESS

Let's keep studying this Woman.

e. **Proverbs 7: 11,12** "*She is loud and stubborn, her feet do not stay in her house.*" This is not a virtue. But looking at it, you learn something very crucial. The seductress is loud and stubborn. She is turbulent and willful. She does everything in her power to get noticed. She does not wait for men to come to her; she goes out to stand on their way to get them. Why is she loud? Because she knows that making yourself noticed is the key to commanding attention. She advertises herself to men. She sells herself to men. They can't help but notice her. Her dressing is loud and absurd. Her makeup is shouting and seductive. Being quiet won't help her. She will just be passed by and forgotten. Why is she stubborn? The word "*stubborn*" originates from the Hebrew word "*Cerar,*" meaning to rebel, be refractory, or revolt. She is a rebel. She does not flow with what is normal; she swims against it. She is unconventional. Not one to submit to patterns and rules. She has a mind of her own. She is like a wild cat, needing to be tamed. She cannot be kept in a home. She is not wife material. She can't stay in a place "her feet abide not in her house" **Proverbs 7:11**.

She is always on the move. Like a huntress, she knows that to catch prey, you can't just sit in the house and wait for it to come knocking on the door; you have to get out there and look for it. To be who she is, she has to rebel against everything she knows to be right. This woman has no conscience. She does not feel remorse when she takes someone's man. To her, it's just business. You must arm yourself for this battle. Don't give her any place at all. Show no mercy, or she will ruin you. She must be stopped!

This book is written so you can get into the mind of the seductress, know her strategies, and arm yourself to resist and overcome her when she manifests, because she will, one day.

f. **Proverbs 7:12** – *"Now is she without, now in the streets and lieth in wait at every corner."* She lies in wait for the cheap prey to fall into her trap. She makes herself seen and noticed. She plants herself on the way, looking for someone to take her. She uses herself as the bait for the man she seeks to catch. She lies in wait. She is also very patient. She can wait. She understands perseverance. She does not sit at home waiting for the man; she goes out where he passes, typically. She knows him and she knows the way he takes and she waits for him there. With her attire carefully designed to entice and entrap, she lures him away from his purpose to her lair. Good men don't wake up in the morning, deciding they will go and chase a woman. They go out to pursue their dreams and purposes. They are usually caught on their way to that designated life pursuit. This seductress simply stands on the way to his pursuit, hoping he might just turn and notice her. One look can be all he needs to turn in or stop for a chat.

She lies in wait at every corner. She hunts for people on the go. If you must catch your man and keep him for life, you must learn this secret. I am not suggesting you should go and stand on the road like a harlot, far from it. I am saying you should know how to position yourself in a place you cannot but be noticed. Know where he is going and plant yourself on his way to that place. Make it look like a chance meeting, a coincidence. Most times, men don't think about women unless these women force their way into their thinking. He is focused on his business, his money, that new job, that promotion, that raise. He is not thinking about a lifelong commitment. So you have to force your way into his thoughts by appearing on his way to his pursuit. The more he sees you, the more he thinks about you. One way to achieve this is to get into his world. What kind of work does he do? Where does he hang out? Which way does he always take? Do your investigation. The seductress catches men by planting herself in their way. She appears in an unusual, different, noticeable, and exotic attire. She trades in spectacles. Colors that attract the eyes. She forces herself into his life in subtle ways, and soon he is the one chasing after her, trying to get her.

g. **Proverbs 7:13** *" So she caught him, and kissed him and with an impudent face said unto him......."*

First of all, let's consider the first phrase in this verse, "so she caught him". This book is about catching your man and keeping him for life. This woman did just that. She caught him. First, she studied him. Understood his wants and desires. His weakness and secret longings. His unfulfilled sexual desires, his hunger for adventure, his little dark secrets.

It is crucial to seek to understand the prey you are trying to catch. She understood him. She knew him. She knew his path. His way. His schedule. His movements. She also knew the kind of person she needed to be to get him; she made herself that, and it was inevitable that he was going to fall for her. Every man has his type of woman.

Most times when a man resists the seduction of a woman, it is because he has everything he wants in the woman he is with, or he does not find the woman attractive. She is not his type. If, for example, he loves busty women and a woman appears with little breasts, that woman will have to work harder to get him. Find out if you are the type of woman he wants. Check the history of the relationships he has had (if any) you will find a pattern. You will notice something all of them have in common. Although some men are hard to study because they don't have a particular taste, most do. The seductress knows all these details, and she uses them to her advantage. **An unsatisfied man is very easy to catch or capture**. But a satisfied man, one who already has in his woman everything he wants, is almost impossible to get. It's like a child who gets all the love and attention from their parents; it's hard to tempt such children with gifts. A child who eats well at home won't go begging for food in his neighbor's house. Contented people are secure people. They are hard to seduce. If you are not the type of "girl" he wants, don't waste your time trying to get him. You will end up the victim at the end of the day. But there is a twist to this: I find some men attracted to a woman not because she is exactly what they want in a woman, not that she is beautiful, but because she possesses certain hidden seductive qualities that they find hard to do without.

Beauty is great, but sometimes it is not enough. You must find a need in his life that only you can meet. It may be an ego need, a need for respect and acceptance. It may be a spiritual need, a need for a deeper experience with someone deep. Or it may be how he likes to be touched. Men are different and come in diverse classes. This is why you must seek to know your prey to know which bait will get him. As we began to see, this seductress caught this man. Next, she does something very strange: "she kissed him....."

Once a man has been caught, anything you do will only heighten the desire and further electrify every moment. Why did she kiss him? Was that not going too far? Wasn't that supposed to make him think how cheap and desperate she was? As I mentioned, she knew him and what he wanted. **A man's desire is his weakness**. It is finding it that is the key. She kissed him to tell him, *"I know who you are on the inside, and I know what you think about and wrestle with all day. I see the way you look at me, and I know you want me as much as I want you. I know what you want and I will give it to you..."* It was more than just a kiss; it was a message. It was a way of communicating with his deepest feelings. Under the spell of that one kiss, his reasoning had been suspended and his mind totally bewitched by her magic. He could no longer think. He had been swept off his feet into a world of fantasies and extreme delight.

A man who can think is very hard to seduce. With a kiss, she stopped his sense of reason. Her spell had been cast. There was no escape. After kissing him, she speaks to him. *"And with an impudent face said unto him..."* All this while she maintains a look on her face. She means business. She had an impudent look on her face. Her gaze was intense and bold. She had that hardened, unashamed expression on her face that told him, *"you are mine now..."* She proved it by kissing him. Her face was stern and serious. This was not a joke. She meant business.

SHE UNDERSTANDS THE POWER OF SACRIFICES

I have peace offerings with me.. This day have I paid my vows. " She is a religious person. She is telling him that finding him was an answered prayer for her.

The word "found" suggests only one thing: she sought after him. This was no accident or chance encounter. This meeting was designed and orchestrated from the very beginning. She paid her vows and gave offerings to catch this man. This is crucial. This was a religious woman. A churchgoer. She understood the mysteries of God. She understood that one of the keys to catching a man was making sacrifices to the gods. She was a giver. She made vows to her god, and she paid them, and behold, a man walks into her territory, totally defenseless and non-resistant. Did her god deliver this man to her? I know not, but somehow she connected her catch with her vow.

This is a secret. To catch your man, you must know how to sow strategic seeds. **"The gift of a man (or woman) maketh way for him..." Proverbs 18:16.** People in the world, when they want to catch a man, go to voodoo doctors (native doctors) and make sacrifices to engage the supernatural in their quest. Somebody is sowing a seed, raising an altar for the man you are trying to catch. It is Seed against Seed. Altar against Altar. Because you are in Christ, you have the advantage. Your sacrifice to Him is more potent than any satanic altar. This woman did not just depend on her beauty to achieve seduction; she also depended on supernatural backing. **"I have this day paid my vows "**

"Therefore came I to meet you, diligently to seek thy face and I have found thee. " This woman is dangerous. She goes to church. She hears the word and she obeys it. She understands the power of sacrificial giving. **She caught this man because she had sown a seed in him.**

What seed have you sown to God for your man? Don't you know that it is only God who can give you your dream man? Without His help, you can do nothing. **John 15:5.** Is anyone threatening your marriage? Take a seed in your hand and engage the God of vengeance on your behalf. Stop appearing before God empty-handed. The people fighting you are fighting you through satanic altars. They are making dangerous sacrifices to catch men. You can't believe what they have to go through to cast a spell on a man. How can you sit and do nothing and expect to win in this battle? It's time to take action. It will be altar against altar. The seductress is a giver. A dangerous giver. She gives to the gods and she gives to men. She knows that the greatest form of seduction is giving. Stinginess repels favor, both from God and men. You can't win this battle, tight-fisted. I know a lady, in her forties she was yet to be married. When she heard me speak on this mystery, without being told, she went and withdrew her life savings to engage God in this battle. She brought it with tears in her eyes and asked me to pray for her. I did. One year later, she got married to her dream man. And what a wedding that was! She caught her man with a sacrifice. "*He that goeth forth and weepeth, bearing precious seed, shall doubtless come again with rejoicing, bringing his sheaves with him.*" **Psalm126:6.** Are you a tither? When you eat your tithe, you rob God. **Malachi 3:8.** Your tithe is ten percent of whatever God brings to you. That 10% belongs to God. It is the Lord's tithe. If you are the type who eats their tithe, you risk a lot of problems. First, it attracts a curse... "*Ye are cursed with a curse; for ye have robbed me, even this whole nation*" **Malachi 3:9.** You don't want any curse to stop your blessing. Paul in **Ephesians 4:27** admonishes us not to give the devil a foothold to use against us. Not paying your tithe can release devourers into your life and relationships. You wonder why you keep giving and doing your best, and still nothing is working? Devourers need to be rebuked. And only God can rebuke them. "*Bring ye all the tithes into the storehouse (God's storehouse is the church where you are nourished and fed with God's word every week. Take your tithe there.) that there may be meat in My house and prove me (Test me, Investigate, Challenge me and Scrutinize me) now herewith, saith the Lord of hosts, if I will not open you the windows of heaven, and pour you a blessing, that there shall not be room enough to receive it...*"

"*And I will rebuke the devourer for your sakes and he shall not destroy the fruits of your grounds, neither shall your vine cast her fruits before the time in the field, saith the Lord of Hosts*" **Malachi 3:10**

This is instructive. There is a reason why your vine is dropping its fruits before its time. This is about the premature ending of

relationships. It starts so well, but then it's suddenly aborted. No wonder people start something, maybe a family, a business, a relationship, and it's so good and promising at the beginning, but suddenly it ends in a bad way. It is a curse. Your tithe is how you engage God to rebuke those evil forces that keep coming back to end your blessing, to steal your miracle. It is time to eliminate the devourer. Repent from not paying your tithe regularly (or at all) and begin today. Something good is about to happen. This seductress never failed to pay her vows. No wonder men kept falling into her hands. Don't be in the habit of making vows before God and not keeping them. Keep your vows even when it hurts. Do it! **Ecclesiastes 5:1 – 7**. *"When thou vowest a vow unto God, defer not to pay it: for He hath no pleasure in fools.*
Pay that which thou hast vowed. Better it is that thou shouldest not vow, than that thou shouldest vow and not pay." Hannah made a vow to God in her barrenness. She vowed to give back to God the son if He gave her one. **1 Samuel 1:11**. God heard that vow and answered her prayer. Are you desperate for a miracle in your relationship? Does it seem like time is running out on you, and nothing seems to be working out? Does it seem to you like your man is being attracted by someone else, and his love for you is fading fast? Do you keep having disappointment after disappointment in your relationships? Do you feel as if some satanic power somewhere is responsible for your relational mishaps? Beauty won't help here, neither will charm. You need a divine intervention. Vow a vow to God. What will you do for Him if He does this for you? To help you do this, I have prepared a little form for you. It is your covenant with God.

FILL THIS FORM

NAME..

......

....

......

AGE..

......

SEX..

OCCUPATION...

PRAYER REQUEST...

....

....

WHAT DO YOU VOW TO DO FOR GOD?.......................

....

....

SIGNATURE...DATE..................

Always refer back to this covenant because God is a God of covenant. He is the one who gives men. *"When the ways of a man pleaseth God, He maketh even his enemies to be at peace with him"* **Proverbs16:7.**

"Delight yourself in the LORD your GOD and He shall give you the desires of your heart." **Psalm 37:4**

"Vow and pay unto the Lord your God: let all that be round about Him bring presents unto Him that ought to be feared. He shall cut off the spirit of princes: He is terrible to the kings of the earth" **Psalm 76:11,12.** God does terrible things in righteousness. Vow and pay. He will destroy every power fighting against your relationship. He will cut them off, and they will cease to exist. Engage God.

This woman teaches us many secrets. **Leviticus 7:11 – 15** talks about the law of peace offerings. This woman knew the law and obeyed it. God cannot be bought by sacrifices, but know that when we, His children, fail to follow His words, we open the door for the enemy to hurt us. We entrust our protection to God, shielding us from those who give to the devil to harm us. While they are making sacrifices to devils to harm us or to take our blessing, let us respond by sowing a battle seed to God to fight for us and save us from them.

SHE IS DILIGENT: SHE MEANS BUSINESS

Having offered and paid her vows, she had the confidence to go in for the kill. *"Therefore come I forth to meet thee and I have found thee..."* **Proverbs 7:15**. She had been looking for him. She was diligent. To catch your man, you can't be a lazy bird, watching TV all day, pressing your phone ad infinitum. Men don't jump out of TV sets! Nor can you download them with your phone. Just like women, they are found. Proverbs 18:22. And I tells us that *"he that seeketh findeth..."* but you must seek diligently. To be diligent means *"shachar"*. To seek early or earnestly, to seek many times. She would get up very early in life to seek her man. Don't wait until it is too late. Start now. Be diligent. Wake up early and get out there, in the marketplace of human affairs, and do your search with the backing of God. She found him, and she caught him, and he was hers.

9. *"I have decked my bed with coverings of tapestry, with carved works, with fine linen of Egypt..."* **Proverbs 7:16**. This woman is detailed. Seduction is very detailed. Everything must be put into consideration. It is when a man notices all the little details, all the little things you had to do to impress him that you knock him off his feet. You may not realize this but he notices every detail. *Your eyes*, the shades, the careful and artful carvings of your *eyebrows*. *Your hair*. How neatly you have done it. *Your dressing*. How clean, how smart, how neat, how sexy. A detailed woman is perceived to be very deep. The seductress knows that catching her man does not totally rely on God. She has to do her part. She has to put up her best act always.

10. *"I have perfumed my bed with myrrh, aloes and cinnamon.."* . Nothing sticks in a man's mind about a woman more than her perfume. Seduction is a peculiar smell. A sweet, mystical fragrance that embodies a goddess. A different and mysterious *"you"*. You can't afford a foul smell. Not even your beauty can atone for that. Ask any man, and they will tell you that what trips them most in a

woman is her perfume. That perfume has a way of carving your image into his subconsciousness: that anywhere he perceives that smell again, you come back to his mind. A good fragrance can work that needed magic. Carefully select what works with your personality. Don't be cheap. A good smell opens the heart and releases favor. Even on God, this mystery works. Why did God regret destroying earth with a flood? What made Him change His mind? A sweet fragrance…." "*And the Lord smelled a sweet savor: and the Lord said in His heart, I will not again curse the ground any more for* man's *sake…*" **Genesis 8:21**. If it can change God's mind, it can change any man. A good perfume provokes favor. You can't smell of heat and sweat and be wondering what is chasing them away. We all have bad odor, especially when we don't clean up and stay fresh. But that is no excuse for carrying bad odor around… "*Because of the savor of thy good ointments, thy name is as ointment poured forth, therefore do the virgins love thee.*" **Songs of Solomon 1:3**. Good odor commands good favor. It is your duty as a woman to smell fresh and sweet always.

For Esther to appear before the King so that he could choose her for his queen, she spent one whole year applying perfume, incense, and fragrances. One whole year! **Esther 2:12** "*Now when every maid's turn was to come to go in to the King Ahasuerus, after that she had been twelve months (1 year) according to the manner of the women for so were the days of their purifications accomplished, to wit, six months with oil and myrrh and six months with sweet odors and with other things for the purifying of the women.*"

When Esther subjected herself to this practice, see what followed: and the King loved Esther above all women and she obtained grace and favor in his sight more than all the virgins, so that he set the royal crown upon her head and made her queen instead of Vashti" **Esther 2:17**. That is how your story will be! Smell good, inside out. Combine it with the smell of a good character, and no virgin will stand where you stand. You will outclass them every time. A pleasing fragrance and a good character will take you places. It will hand over kings to your hand. Practice this principle of seduction. The seductress knew men. She knew that a sweet perfume can hold captive the heart of the mightiest. In choosing a good perfume, be moderate, don't overdo it. That, too, can be a turn-off.

11. *"With her much fair speech she caused him to yield, with the flattering of her lips she forced him…"* Seduction revolves around the power of persuasion. Seduction is what you say and how you say it. This seductress knows the power of words. With words even a nation can be taken. Her speech was fair. The Hebrew meaning of "her much fair speech" is *"leqach"*. It means "learning, teaching, insight, teaching–power, persuasiveness, doctrine." This woman was not a novice. She was learned. Her words were rich with "wisdom and insights". She could persuade an army to turn against its commander. She could use her knowledge to her advantage. She was no novice. She read a lot of books and had a lot of information to share. There was something about her that caught the young man's attention – her deep learning and understanding. She could dissect knowledge and put them so graphically that he could see it so clearly. Timidity and ignorance are anti-seduction. To catch the man and keep him, you must know something. How many books have you read this year? What do you know? Beauty is great but it is not enough. *You gotta have brains.* This seductress wasn't some cheap tramp on the way side, she was a woman of knowledge. A learned person. She could engage in productive and mind-tasking conversation without seeming out of touch or ignorant. This is very crucial. Make it a point of duty to learn something about everything. Art, science, religion, politics, fashion, poetry, wars, history, money etc. She caused him to yield to her by her great learning. To be a leader commanding an army of followers, knowledge is your greatest asset. People follow and yield to people who know more than they do. So do men. They find women of great learning beautiful and seductive. He yielded to her deep learning and teaching power. He bowed to her depth of understanding. He couldn't resist her. Don't play with your education. Attend yourself to much learning. It is never a wasted effort. While you are clothing yourself physically with beautiful things, clothe yourself mentally with knowledge. She didn't only

teach him, she also flattered him. She used words that did not wound his ego but instead boosted it. *"With the flattering of her lips, she forced him."* Words are forces. They can compel action. Her words forced him to act. There is a way to talk to a man, and he will do what he never intended to do. He was truly captivated by her eloquence and depth of knowledge.

A woman who can talk can keep a man for life. Now, there is a difference between talking and chattering. It's all in the substance. In countless situations, embracing silence can prove far more valuable than endlessly chattering like a parrot! But when you speak, let wisdom, insight, and learning flow from your lips each time you open your mouth. Mix it with smoothness, sweetness, and softness. *"a soft tongue breaketh the bones"* **Proverbs 25:15.** It breaks the resistance. Impact knowledge with softness and even the strongest will fall at your feet, needing more.

12. *"He goeth after her straightaway, as an ox goeth to the slaughter..* **Proverbs 7:27.** When you have done your work well, you will not need to chase after him; he will go after you. After she finished with him, she turned her back and walked away. She did not hold him or drag him. Her charm had been cast. Her spell was fully tied around his neck. He was hers. All she had to do was walk and have him follow her. Seduction aims to make him chase you. The more he chases you, the more power you have. The key is to make him think he is taking the initiative while you are being elusive. That scenario is powerful. You have caught your man. Now keep him.

FINAL WORD

When he doesn't want to be kept

This book is for women who want to attract and keep the right kind of man, not Mr Wrong. Mr. Wrong is the type of man you should never try to catch or keep. A man who wants to be kept will be grateful to be in your life, while a man who does not wish to be kept cannot be held onto. Don't waste your time with the wrong man; he will take everything you have—your love, emotions, time, precious years, and sometimes even your money. He will squander these gifts and then discard you.

This book aims to help you avoid wasting time with the wrong man. Instead, it focuses on identifying the right man for you and positioning yourself so that he initiates the chase and chooses to keep you. Mr. Wrong will break your heart; he will never love you in the way you deserve. You will never feel enough for him, and he may continue to cheat on you because you are not the woman he wants. Sometimes, this situation worsens even if you marry him.

A man who does not wish to be kept by a woman cannot be kept. Cut your losses and let him go; throw that wrong fish back into the sea because he's not what you're looking for. The man who wants to be with you will make the effort; he will chase after you if you follow the guidance in this book. He will struggle to live without you. That is the man you want—the one who desires you more than you desire him.

If you've caught the wrong fish by mistake, it's okay. Unhook it and throw it back into the river. The right fish will find you, and you won't need to do everything written in this book to catch and keep him; you will simply be the woman of his dreams.

How to Identify Mr. Wrong

Please read the chapter on the 15 types of men you don't want to catch and refresh your mind about these toxic personalities—avoid them. Also, review the chapter that discusses the type of men you should be looking for to help you recognize the right one for you. By doing so, you will make the right choice. This is my prayer for you, in Jesus' name, Amen.

Conclusion

Everything cannot be said in one book. So I have decided to add a sequel to this book. I am presently working on the next volume of this essential material.

Please write me an email and send your comments, contributions, and questions. These will help me in my research as I strive to present a befitting sequel to this groundbreaking book.

My email address is emmannaji2@gmail.com

If you need counseling, prayers, and further guidance on this subject, don't fail to reach out. I am here to serve you.

Tell a friend about the book. It will be a blessing to them, as I am sure it has been to you. Watch out for the 2nd volume.

"Women who conquered Men and their secrets".

. One of the secrets of Esther in the bible was that she had a Mordecai. A Spiritual father. A Mentor. A Leader. Connect with my relationship mentorship classes for more support. Please send me an email on how to join our community..

If you are already hooked to a man, continue to apply these principles, and God will continue to give you victory. Remember, with God, all things are possible.

Is your heart broken? Has someone taken advantage of your love and sincerity only to dash it to the ground? Not to worry, your recovery has begun. With this book, you will soon have the upper hand. Read it, discuss it with friends and loved ones. Discuss it with your sisters' group and above all, do as it says. With time, you will see how the tables have turned and you have begun to call the shots. It is a new day for you. Cheer up, my sister. You will surely smile again.

Don't forget to leave me a review on Amazon!

Thank you so much for choosing to read this book! If it resonated with you, I would be incredibly grateful if you could take just thirty seconds to leave a review on Amazon. Your support means the world to me!

179